Mr. Right Now

Mr. Right Now

Monica Jackson

KENSINGTON PUBLISHING CORP.
http://www.kensingtonbooks.com

DAFINA BOOKS are published by

Kensington Publishing Corp.
850 Third Avenue
New York, NY 10022

All Kensington titles, imprints and distributed lines are available at special quantity discounts for bulk purchases for sales promotion, premiums, fund-raising, educational or institutional use.

Special book excerpts or customized printings can also be created to fit specific needs. For details, write or phone the office of the Kensington Special Sales Manager: Kensington Publishing Corp., 850 Third Avenue, New York, NY 10022. Attn. Special Sales Department. Phone: 1-800-221-2647.

Dafina Books and the Dafina logo Reg. U.S. Pat. & TM Off.

ISBN 0-7582-0867-7

First Kensington Trade Paperback Printing: December 2005
10 9 8 7 6 5 4 3 2 1

Printed in the United States of America

To my daughter, Amethyst

PART ONE

He took my breath and my heart too.
—Luby

Chapter 1

I am black, but comely . . .
—Song of Songs, 1:5

My life changed the day I walked into the elevator of my apartment building behind a tall, young white man, who held a small box of books. I pushed the button, drew in a sharp breath as I realized dampness was collecting between my legs as they grew weak with sexual arousal. I craned my neck and darted a glance at him. His eyes met mine for a split second, a green glint, then desire hit me like a splash of steamy water. My God, I wanted him.

I bit my lower lip to keep from licking it. I wanted to reach out and touch him so much, I curled my right hand into a fist. What was going on?

I never noticed any man in the elevator before. I never wanted to throw any man up against the wall and grind my body against his.

I never looked at another stranger's face and memorized his features at a glance. His hair was dark brown, a little too long. His face was lean and chiseled, his cheeks covered with stubble. Peaked brows hovered over the greenest eyes I'd ever seen.

Close to his body, he held a box that appeared to be filled with old books. He stared up at the numbers that flickered at the passing floors.

The aura of sex and passion that almost visibly rolled from his body was overwhelming in this small space. It took all my self-control not to hit the button that stopped the elevator and beg him to take me.

Instead, I bit my lower lip harder between my teeth. So hard, I wouldn't have been surprised to feel warm blood. He gave me a nervous glance as if he knew exactly the effect he was having. Then he said, "Maybe I should have taken the stairs."

Saliva trickled down my throat with my gasp of shock. I coughed and sputtered. He steadied me with a touch that made my arousal increase.

"I'm sorry, what did you say?" I got the words out with difficulty.

He looked guilty. "My name is Jake Kosevo. I recently moved into the building."

"Luby Jones," I mumbled, not able to meet his eyes, because of the thick heat trickling between my legs. "Welcome."

The elevator doors opened. "This is my floor," he said. "Nice to meet you."

He'd started out of the elevator and the box suddenly gave way and books tumbled everywhere. He swore something in a language I didn't recognize.

I tried not to gasp when I saw the titles of the books. There were words like "magic" and "sorcery" in them, one even said "demonology." A shiver of fear went through me.

"Will you hold the elevator button for me while I gather these?" he asked.

I stabbed at the open button with a stiff finger while he scrambled to collect his books. I tried hard not to breathe or

4

look at his rear end. Did I mention that his voice was wonderful, totally masculine, like rough, dark silk?

It obviously had been way too long since I'd been with a man.

"Let me help you carry them to your place." The words tumbled out of my mouth. I almost clapped my hand to my mouth in astonishment. Did I invite myself to the man's apartment? A man for whom I felt I'd barter with the devil for his touch?

"I appreciate it," he said.

I stumbled behind him through his door, awkwardly holding onto an armful of books whose titles scared me half to death. Apparently fear didn't affect my sex drive, because my gaze fastened to his rear like it was glued when he bent over to pile the books on the floor.

"I'll take those," he said, reaching for the books. His closeness flustered me so much I almost dropped them.

I dragged my gaze from his body and looked around his apartment. He had no furniture and what looked like a sleeping bag lay in the middle of the floor.

"Thanks a lot," he said.

"It's okay." I'd never seen a porn movie in my life, but imagined naughty scenarios that ended up with me bare-assed on the floor were flitting through my mind.

Inner alarms rang. "Um, I better get going," I said, edging toward the door. "Nice to meet you. Welcome to the building." Then before I could shame myself, I wheeled and fled.

Back at my apartment, I sank to the sofa without kicking off my shoes the way I usually do. My mouth was dry, and dampness was still sticky between my thighs.

The phone rang.

"Luby, can I borrow your car?" Danni asked. "I need to take Allen to a birthday party in an hour."

"What happened to your car?"

"Marcus took it."

"You're joking. You allowed that rusty Negro to take your car when you know you needed to take your son out tonight?" I asked. What was the matter with that girl? She was addicted to a certain type of man and too much of her brain was wired between her legs. The thought reminded me of Jake.

"I didn't *let* Marcus take my car, he took it on his own."

An idea lit up in my head. There was no way that guy was for me and Danni needed help in the man department in a major way. He'd probably never be attracted to a black woman, and to be frank, he wasn't what I wanted either. But he'd be perfect for Danni. He definitely had the sex appeal to make her forget about that sorry Marcus.

Danni liked black men and black men only, although she was a petite, pretty blonde with a generous chest and big blue eyes. I know, once you go black, you don't go back, but it was deeper than that. She had issues and apparently sleeping with black men helped.

Most white girls like that were subconscious racists wanting only to degrade themselves, but I'd known Danni long enough to see she didn't have a bigoted bone in her body. Once I'd suggested therapy and she went off on me.

But it wasn't that she liked the brothers that bothered me; it was the sort of brother she went for. Danni always ended up with thugs, dangerous thugs.

She'd get her heart beaten down, her apartment ripped off, and niggas hanging around who knew to the minute when her paycheck was coming.

Danni needed help. I had to figure out a way to hook her up with Jake.

"I have a guy I want you to meet," I said.

"Marcus and I—"

6

"Are a train wreck. C'mon, this guy is fine." Danni had a thing for luscious babes and the babe on the elevator was as luscious as they come.

"Mmmmm, what's his build?"

"Just how you like 'em, tall and built, but lean."

"Is he light or dark-skinned?"

There it was. Danni wasn't asking if he were white or black, she was asking about skin tone. She assumed I'd hook her up with a brother. I knew she'd have a fit once she saw Jake was white, because she had let me know several times that she was a woman of definite tastes.

I took the cowardly way out. "He's light-skinned," I said.

"Okay, when, where and how?" Danni asked with a sigh of resignation.

"I'm not sure yet, but when I am, you'll promise to meet him?"

"Sure," she said, relief in her voice.

"C'mon and get the car keys then."

"Thanks, Luby. You're the best friend ever."

"Yeah, yeah." I didn't want to dwell on how much of my motivation to fix Danni up was because I wanted to have a reason to see Jake again.

I hung up the phone feeling uneasy. I wasn't tripping over that guy, was I? My grandmother didn't raise that kind of fool.

I was restless inside. Dissatisfied. Maybe we're creatures with finite timetables after all, and Grandma was right about mine running out.

I was twenty-six years old and I'd been out of law school for two years. I believed that my job, my friends, the church, Grandma, and the occasional date were enough. Like a lot of other people I knew, I thought Mr. Right was out there, and he'd find me eventually. I'd never felt the keen edge of need for a man before. Maybe it was past time.

I reached out and picked up the newspaper from the couch. I turned the pages, unseeing, while I considered my options.

I went to church every Sunday, was active in the choir and the woman's group, and traveled to fellowship with other churches whenever I had the opportunity.

The good Christian man I'd hoped for never materialized. I wanted a professional, educated man, but most important, I wanted a man with Christian principles. I wanted a man who was a pillar of the church and his community. A strong black man whom I could lean on and trust.

But there were a whole lot of sisters like me, looking for exactly the same brother.

I needed my yellow silk shirt to go with the navy blue suit I wanted to wear to work tomorrow. I'd lent it to Cat and she never gives anything back.

I knocked on the door, and Cat opened it, putting her finger to her lips so I'd be quiet. Her husband Darryl was asleep on the couch in front of the television with ESPN on. A fine line of saliva ran from his mouth and down his chin.

She motioned me into the kitchen. I'd known both Danni and Cat for the six years we'd all lived in the building. We paid primo rent in one of the high rises near the Plaza, but for me, it was worth it. I thought the area was one of the best things about Kansas City.

Folks often mistook Cat and I for sisters because we're both small, exactly the same height and frame, but Cat was slimmer. She said she wished she had my tits and ass, and sometimes I wished I had her size four.

Cat has slanty hazel eyes that were a legacy from some unknown white folks, along with light golden skin. She'd told me her natural hair was kinky and short, burned off by relaxers, but her weave was a fabulous one, her hair looked straight, long, black, and shiny.

Her full name was Catherine Maria Bronson-Harris, a kindness compared to my Luby Uniquoncie Jones. My mother must have hated me at birth.

Cat opened the refrigerator door and put a cold beer in my hand. "There was this babe in the hallway," she said. "He was so hot, it was fuckin' incredible. My panties are still damp."

"Jake, right?" I said.

"You know him?"

"I met him in the elevator the other day. He's . . . quite amazing."

"He was lucky I didn't rape him on the spot," Cat said.

"Me too," I said, staring off into the distance.

Cat choked on her beer. "What did you say?"

I laughed, tickled. Cat thought I was such a Goody Two-Shoes. "I said, me too."

"Damn, girl, what is with that guy?" Cat asked. "I've seen good-looking guys before, but shit."

"I was thinking he'd be perfect for Danni," I said.

Cat's eyes narrowed. "She doesn't like white guys."

"She doesn't like her yearly pelvic exam either, but it's good for her. You know she should be doing better."

"Shouldn't we all?" Cat said, taking a sip of beer.

"You have to admit, Danni's pathetic. A pretty, slim white girl, living the same hell as a hefty sista."

Cat laughed. "Could be poetic justice."

"Nah, we should save her from her own silly self."

"And a fine white boy is going to do it?" Cat asked.

"It's a start," I said.

"How are we going to set them up?"

"I'm not sure."

9

Cat shook her head. "You're all talk and no action."

Cat got out a skillet, set it on the stove and opened the refrigerator. I settled back on the stool and sipped my beer, enjoying the company. I was in no rush to collect my shirt.

"Fuck!" Cat suddenly yelled.

I flinched. "What's wrong with you?" I asked her.

She glared into the refrigerator. "The hamburger I put in the refrigerator to thaw this morning is gone. Goddamn. Darryl!"

"Darryl!" she yelled again, an octave higher.

"What is it?" His voice was sleepy and irritated, but not nearly as irritated as Cat.

"What did you do with the hamburger in the refrigerator?"

"Uh, I was hungry."

Cat slammed the refrigerator door shut. I stood up, figuring it was time I headed home. She stalked into the living room. I decided to stay in the kitchen until the worst of it blew over.

"You ate a whole pound of hamburger? What the fuck is wrong with you? I was planning on making spaghetti for dinner."

"Cook something else."

"Everything else is frozen. Looks like you're going to be taking me out to eat."

"I'm tired, Cat."

"Doing what? You ain't done shit all day."

Darryl was a firefighter. He worked one day on, where he was at the station for twenty-four hours, and two days off. Cat worked nine to five as a copywriter in a company that put out trade magazines by the dozen. She didn't like her job much.

"Motherfucker, you were home all day, why didn't you get off your lazy ass and clean the house and cook dinner!" Cat screamed.

I guessed now rather than later would be a good time to leave.

"Bitch, please," Darryl said.

10

Oh no, he didn't say that. I darted toward the door, and closed it behind me before the hell I knew was coming broke out. They didn't even notice me in the heat of their battle. I'd call Cat later and ask her to bring my shirt. The more I looked at Cat and Darryl, the more it looked as if the state of marriage was way overrated.

I trekked down to the laundry room late Friday night. It was a time when I could usually count on it being empty. I could also usually count on my not having a date.

I felt his presence before I saw him. I know that sounds corny, but it was true. Jake crouched on the floor, struggling to open a gigantic box of Tide.

Dammit, I wanted to rip that white boy's pants clean off. What was going on with me?

CHAPTER 2

Draw me, we will run after thee . . .
  —Song of Songs, 1:4

I loaded my clothes in the dryer and tried to look at him out of the corner of my eye without turning my head. There was a foreign air about him, along with something soulful and melancholy in his light eyes. I could tell he had secrets.

I inhaled and let it out slow. Dang, he was fine. "Hi. Need some help with that big box of detergent?" I asked.

He looked up and smiled at me. I damn near fainted. "Luby," he said. "Good to see you again."

He remembered my name. He stood and my skin started burning along with everything else down there. I thought I was the type to need some direct action to go with visuals before I could get turned on to this extent. But merely being in the same room with this man was setting me on fire.

"I think I've got it," he said as he found the tag that allowed him to rip the box top open. "Do you think liquid is better than powder?" he asked.

"I always use liquid, mainly because it's easier to carry." I twirled my hair with my index finger. My hormones had moved in and taken over my brain completely.

"Choice of detergent must be habit. We always used powder back home, so I grabbed this gigantic box," he said.

"You recently moved here?" I asked.

"Yeah. I came in from out of state."

I retreated to the far end of the small laundry room and started throwing my clothes into a washer. Jake overwhelmed me. He looked cosmopolitan and sophisticated, despite his scruffy dress. He probably moved from New York or somewhere like that. "Where are you from?" I asked.

"Montana. My family has a ranch there."

My eyebrows shot up. Montana? A rural type? Unbelievable. He looked dark, lean, foreign and intense. He was the dead opposite of sunny, corn-fed and content Montana ranchers I'd imagined, or even a dark and dangerous cowboy type.

There was something sophisticated and world-weary about him. He had eyes that looked as if they'd seen all. There was sadness about him that gave him a devastating little boy charm. *Can I take care of you, baby? I'll make you happy.*

I twisted my mind away from my musing and lascivious thoughts and searched for witty repartee. "So what brings you to Kansas City? Your job?" I asked, the witty repartee part of my brain failing miserably.

"I needed a change."

I waited but that was all he was going to say.

He glanced at me and I swallowed hard. Moistening my lips, I summoned my courage to ask him, "I'm having a few friends over for dinner tomorrow. Why don't you drop by and meet some of your neighbors?"

There. I did it.

He smiled like the sun rising between my thighs. "I'd like that," he said.

"Is seven-thirty all right? I'm in apartment 512."

"It's fine."

"Well, see you then. I better go." I wheeled and fled as if a pack of demon hounds were behind me, leaving my clothes abandoned in the washer.

I'd get them later. Way later. Maybe tomorrow.

I always went to Grandma's on Saturday morning and took her shopping. She still lived in the same house I grew up in, with white siding and a small yard that we kept filled with flowers in the spring and summer, I loved coming home on Saturdays to my good childhood memories.

But as soon as I walked into the house that morning, Grandma reminded me of a particularly bad memory. "I heard from your mother," she said.

I frowned. "What's the matter?"

"The home says she needs some more underwear and nightgowns. We'll pick some up when we're out and run by to drop them off."

I didn't say anything, but a little tremor ran through me. I hated going to see my mother and my grandmother knew it. There must be a reason she was making me take her instead of going during the week as she usually did.

"You want some pie?"

"That sounds wonderful."

A few minutes later, I settled at the old kitchen table with cherry pie and milk.

Grandma sat across from me.

"I should have had this talk with you a while ago," she said.

I was alarmed. Those were the same words she used to open the birds and bees talk years ago.

"In several months you'll be twenty-seven, nine times three. It's a sacred number."

"Uh-huh."

She sighed and played with her fork. "That was the age when your mother changed." She paused. "When I changed."

"Grandma, what is your point? Changed how?" I didn't mean to be impatient, but dang.

"For you, I'm not sure."

My alarm increased. Maybe Grandma was getting Alzheimer's disease. She'd been complaining about how forgetful she was getting.

"For me, I started knowing about things. Things that were going to happen, baby."

My heart started to pound. *Grandma, no.*

"Your mother heard the dead. It was too much for her, tipped her totally over the edge. My baby's head had never been screwed on that tight anyway," she muttered.

Well, insanity ran in the family, I thought with dread, thinking about my mother.

"You're looking at me like I'm crazy. I knew you would," Grandma said. "But when you turn twenty-seven, everything changes. I can't explain how, but I thought you should know. Prepare yourself."

She looked out the picture window that spilled buttery morning sun and peered at the luxurious flower beds we'd planted together. "They called your great-grandmother a witch. She healed people with herbs for a fee. But she told me once that the herbs were for show, that she didn't need them."

She focused on my face and smiled. "Finish your pie. The world isn't coming to an end. There's a sale at Sears."

16

I lifted my fork. A lot of families have weird legends. That's what it was. I have a crazy mother. It would be mighty hard if my grandmother went crazy too, but I'd deal with it, because unlike my mother, I knew that Grandma loved me.

Grandma bought what she needed from Sears, and wanted to go straight to see my mother, Lily. I drove her there and started to pull a book out of my purse as Grandma climbed out of the front seat. It was hot as hell out here, but I'd wait. I hated going in there, it felt like a warehouse of empty bodies. It was laid out like a nursing home, but instead of the elderly, it housed people too crazy to fend for themselves.

"Aren't you coming in?" Grandma asked.

"I'll wait."

"You need to come in today," she said.

I bit my lip and my hand tightened on my book.

"You need to come in, now," Grandma said again. She had that familiar look on her face that told me she wasn't taking no for an answer and she wasn't taking any crap or backtalk either.

I got out of the car.

We walked into the dingy room my mother shared with another woman. She was alone, staring at the television. Grandma would have kept Lily at home, but when I was a child Lily threw herself through the picture window, and did other things my grandmother wouldn't speak of.

"Lily," Grandma said, sitting beside her. "We brought you the things you need."

Mother sat up with a quick motion, still lithe. She gave a nod in my direction, but wouldn't look at me.

"Good," she said.

The medications made her eyes dull and vacant, as if her soul

17

had vacated. Her lips moved constantly, as if speaking to unseen companions.

My skin crawled. Grandma believed my mother actually talked to the dead? That they were here, surrounding her?

That thought led to places I didn't want to go. Too much craziness, too much pain.

Grandma sat on the bed beside her daughter.

"I'm going to go and talk to the nurse," I said.

"Stay," Grandma said. I tightened my lips and sank into a chair on the other side of the room, while Grandma drew each item from the shopping bag in turn and showed it to Lily.

I was happy that my mother didn't look at me, because ever since I could remember, my mother looked at me with hatred in her eyes.

I was told that after my mother became pregnant, my father disappeared and she never saw him again. It was a vague, unsatisfying story but all that Grandma offered me.

Grandma did try to explain my mother's antipathy toward me. She said my mother hated her body swelling with pregnancy, hating the little parasite that latched on to her, feeding, needing. Grandma said Lily hated my father and hated me because I looked like him, walked like him, talked like him and even smelled like him.

I couldn't understand my mother's hatred of me as a child. Plenty of my friends had no-good fathers, but their mothers didn't hate them. Didn't my mother realize that it wasn't my fault who I looked like? I would have looked like her if I could because there are few things harder for a child to endure than their mother's hatred.

Grandma was my shield, my sheltering rock. When Lily was sent away, all I felt was relief.

Grandma cried when Lily left. I know she felt bad that she

couldn't save her daughter, but she saved me. Wasn't that enough?

I grew up, but my mother's hatred remained, sane or not. What fault was it of mine who she chose to spread her legs for before I was born?

My mother's hatred burned a hole into me, and any love that I could have felt for her fell into it, gone into the void. Grandma told me to ask the Lord to give me the strength to accept what I couldn't change.

"They told me that the little bitch met him," Lily said to Grandma. I flinched, startled. Little bitch was her favorite word to describe me. But she hadn't referred to me directly in years. Who did she mean by "him?"

Grandma said nothing and didn't look at me.

"You wanted to fuck him, didn't you, little bitch?" Lily asked. My God, was she speaking about Jake? No. She couldn't be.

"And you will. Be careful, little bitch, because it'll be the death of you." She sniffed, her mouth moving, her eyes fastened on something I couldn't see.

I stood, feeling tiny hairs rise on the back of my arms. Grandma still looked down on the faded coverlet, but then she *nodded* as if in agreement.

I couldn't take an instant more. I turned and fled from the room.

I stood outside taking deep gulps of air, downwind of the residents who smoked one cigarette after another. A few minutes later, my pounding pulses stilled, I moved to the car.

It was like a furnace. I rolled down the windows and turned the ignition, flipping the AC up to full blast.

She couldn't be talking about Jake. It was impossible. But I'd never met any man before who moved me so strongly. *You*

19

wanted to fuck him, didn't you, little bitch? I did. Yes, Lily . . . Mother, I did.

The air cooled and I rolled up my windows, locked the doors and leaned my forehead against the steering wheel, and waited. *She hears dead people,* Grandma said. *I know about things. Things that are going to happen, baby.*

I could deal with a lot. I considered myself a strong woman. But this was outside my ken. Madness ran in the family, and I didn't have much family to lose. Tears stung my eyes. At twenty-seven was I going to turn stark raving bonkers? Was that it?

It was an hour later when Grandma tapped on the car window, looking tired and older, as if her daughter had drained her of years.

I unlocked the door and she got in heavily. When I pulled away, she said, "Luby, if you keep love in your heart, you'll never turn out like your mother."

Was that the message she'd been trying to give me? I'd decided in those long minutes while I waited that losing my marbles wasn't a possibility. I was rooted in reality, and in reality was where I'd stay. I murmured something unintelligible. It must have satisfied her, because she let the topic go.

CHAPTER 3

Let my beloved come into his garden . . .
—Song of Songs, 4:16

I called in five pizzas from Grandma's for carryout and picked them up on the way home along with plenty of six packs of ice-cold beer. I'd add a salad as a token toward veggies and health that everyone would ignore and we were good to go for my little get-together.

My stomach was churning with anticipation. I was going to see Jake, up close and personal. I needed to chill out. He wasn't for me. I wasn't his type and he wasn't mine, but he was the answer to Danni's prayers even if she didn't know it yet.

I had to make three trips to get all the food and drinks up to my apartment. Cat once told me that she pegged me to be the type to have everything in my place covered in plastic, curtains with tiny floral patterns and ornate Victorian furniture.

No way. I'd filled my entire apartment with plants and they gave off a fresh green odor. My walls were covered with African masks and on the floor were piles of bright pillows covered with gauzy Indian fabric with sparkly threads and shiny bits of mirror and gilt. I like simple, soft and overstuffed furniture in bright

21

colors too. Everybody commented how my apartment was so unlike me, but they couldn't be more wrong. My apartment was who I really was.

There was a rap on the door. "Lemme in," Cat said.

"It's open."

Cat bounced in and looked around. "What's cooking?"

Then she spied the pizza on the coffee table. "Men like pizza. That'll work."

"You're right in time to help me make the salad," I said.

"But you said that you had a one-ass kitchen, and I should keep my ass out of it while you're in it."

I laughed. "It is a one-ass kitchen, but get yours in there and make a spinach salad because I need to shower and change. Boiled eggs are in the fridge. Put lots of mushrooms in it, okay?"

"What if Jake doesn't like mushrooms?"

"Then I assume he won't eat the salad. We love mushrooms." I wasn't about to make such sacrifices even for the sexiest man I'd ever laid eyes on in my life.

I went into my bedroom and took off my shorts. I dug around in my underwear drawer until I found the thong I'd bought but never had the nerve to wear, and laid it out on the bed with a short denim skirt and a matching halter. Carefully putting my shower cap on so my pressed hair wouldn't get wet and frizz, I adjusted the water temperature, then sighed in satisfaction as I climbed in.

My strange sexual attraction to Jake had to be hormone fluctuations. Maybe time-of-the-month weirdness. It was nothing to worry about. Things would go great tonight. Cat's husband was coming later. I asked Winston from the office too. Winston was handsome and good company, and gay as Sponge Bob.

It would be obvious that Jake was partnered with Danni. I'd reminded her of her promise to get her to say she'd show this evening, but her word was good. Our mutual neighbor, Mrs. Thompson, said Danni had asked her to babysit this evening.

I was feeling almost saintly about my crusade to help Danni. She was raised middle-class in upscale Johnson County suburbs and wasn't drugged or thugged out, so it was a mystery why she put up with the crap.

A single parent of an eight-year-old biracial son, she worked long hours on her feet as an LPN. Danni had a far harder life than a pretty white girl should have.

I heard Cat talking, and I turned off the shower. It must be Danni. I dried off and smoothed lotion into my skin.

"What's wrong?" Cat asked Danni.

"Marcus took my car," she said.

I rolled my eyes. Again?

"You let that fool drive your car?" Cat asked.

"He took my keys."

I shook my head as I drew on my underwear. The girl was hopeless.

I heard a tap at the door. I pulled my halter top on. "Come on in," I said.

Danni and Cat both came in and sat on the bed. I moved to the dresser and picked up my blush, my back to them.

"Did you call the police?" I asked Danni.

"Please. Marcus will be back," she said.

"Danni, he stole your car. You got a kid and you can't do without a car. What if he doesn't come back?"

"He'll be back," she repeated. "Tomorrow's Saturday, so I'll be all right." She glanced at my reflection in my dresser mirror. "He's on probation. If I call the police, they'll throw him in jail."

"So? It seems like that's where his ass needs to be," Cat said.

Danni sighed and flopped back on the bed.

Lord.

"Who else is coming?" Danni asked.

"Winston, Darryl, and this new guy who moved into the building."

"Couples. This guy better be decent or I'm kicking your ass."

Danni wasn't dumb. Her problem was that she thought with her cooch, instead of her brain cells.

"Like you don't need somebody else after that worthless SOB stole your car?" Cat said.

"You've seen this guy?" Danni asked her.

Cat darted a glance at me. "I saw him once."

"So, what's he look like?"

Cat hesitated. "He looks damn good," she answered.

I finished with my mascara and stepped back to study the results.

"You look great," Cat said. "You're really much prettier than me."

"I'd kill for your skin," Danni added.

Cat and I both laughed simultaneously. "Nope, Danni, you don't need to add to your problems."

"You two look good. Luby, I haven't seen you show so much thigh since forever. This guy that moved in must be something else," Danni said.

She was telling no lie, I thought. The intercom buzzed and I rushed to it, glad not to have to answer her.

"I'm hungry, girlfriend, let me up," Winston said.

I buzzed him in. There was a knock on the door as soon as I stepped away from the intercom.

I pulled open the door and my stomach flipped as I looked into Jake's glittering green eyes.

I licked my lips and wished they were his. "Welcome," I said, standing aside.

His smile reached down so deep, I realized with dismay that if

24

my irrational sexual response to him was my hormones, they were still way out of whack.

"Don't shut the door on me, girl," Winston said from behind Jake.

"Can I get you a Heineken?" I asked Jake, needing to leave the room, to get away from him if only for a moment so I could pull myself together.

"That would be great."

"Did you forget my existence, Ms. It?" Winston asked querulously, sounding gay as hell.

"No, Winston, dear. I'll get you a beer too."

"That's more like it," he said. "And who is this?" Winston asked. I swear he batted his eyelids at the man.

"Winston James, this is Jake—uh . . ." My mind went blank and his last name skittered away.

"Jacob Kosevo," he said, proffering his hand to Winston. "Everybody calls me Jake."

Winston perked up, and held Jake's hand a moment too long. I noticed his eyes drop to the bulge in Jake's jeans. Winston's such a slut.

"Jake this is my friend Cat, her husband Darryl should be here shortly."

Cat actually fluttered her hands as she mumbled something unintelligible. I noticed that she couldn't meet Jake's eyes.

I turned to Danni. Danni was obviously in shock, with flags of red at her cheeks and her eyes bright. "Jake, this is Danielle Sellers, but we call her Danni." I turned away from her, bitch that I've become. "Help me with the beer won't you?" I purred to Jake.

"No, I will." Danni found her voice and dragged me into the kitchen. I was almost relieved to be saved from my awry hormones. Almost.

"Sheesh," Danni said. "Sheesh. He's so beautiful. I think I want to marry him. Is he a god down from Olympus?"

I shook my head no, but I couldn't bring myself to disagree, because the man was a serious hottie. I'd never thought in a million years I'd be in danger of losing my mind over a white guy. "Pull yourself together and go out there and do your best to impress," I said, eyeing her blonde hair and blue eyes with momentary envy. But some things were for the best, I mentally kicked myself.

"I need to ask you something," Danni asked.

I leaned against the counter feeling nervous at the seriousness of Danni's tone. "Luby, I figured you were setting me up with a white guy." Danni frowned. "Be honest. Are you one of those who think the races should never mingle?"

I sighed. Was that all she was going to say? I thought she was going to go off on me. "I don't have anything against interracial relationships," I said. "But to be frank, I don't think *you* should mingle. You scrape the bottom of the barrel, girl. If you were dating classy black guys who treat you well, that would be one thing. What you do is another. Maybe you should try out a different sort of man."

She shook her head. "I've been mingling since I was sixteen when I gave it up to the fine basketball player after the prom." She made a slight grimace. "I must say I was disappointed. I'd heard so much about black men. But thank God, since then I've had far better."

I swear Danni cracked me up.

The phone rang. "Get out there and do the hostess thing for me," I said to Danni before I picked up.

"Luby? This is Darryl. Uh, can I speak to Cat? Never mind, Luby, hold up. Just tell her I can't come. I'm sorry, but something came up, aw'raht?"

26

I hung up shaking my head. "Cat, c'mere," I called. She walked into the kitchen, hands on hips, chin thrust out. "Darryl?" she asked.

"He said he can't make it."

Cat's eyes narrowed and she headed straight to the phone. I thought it wise to decamp, and sure enough, a few seconds later, I heard her raised, angry voice. It didn't sound as if she was sweet-talking Darryl into coming.

Jake was looking through my DVDs and everybody else was looking at Jake.

"Help yourself to the pizza," I said. "There's napkins and paper plates on the dining room table. Danni, could you put on a DVD or some music or something? Maybe there's something Jake wants to hear. I'm going to check on Cat."

I moved quickly to the kitchen. It was way too quiet, and quiet wasn't natural for Cat.

Cat was leaning with her face against the wall. I touched her shoulder. "Can I help?"

"You wanna kill Darryl for me?" She laughed, a sound so bitter it was scary. "I swear I can't stand Darryl most of the time."

My pulses quickened. Cat was rarely this open. Worse, she looked depressed on top of upset. That wasn't like her, either. Her husband was fine, kept a good job and stayed at home nights. Lord, if that wasn't enough, what was?

"Danni's one lucky bitch," she said. "I'd like to fuck that white boy until he loses his mind."

I raised an eyebrow. What a change of subject. That was more like her.

"Don't worry, I won't," she added.

"He may not like her," I said.

"White boys always like her. She's gorgeous, and she's skinny with big tits."

27

I nodded. Danni had confided that her parents paid for her boob job for a sweet-sixteen gift.

"She's a short, blonde Barbie," Cat said.

Yeah, white guys tended to go gonzo over Danni right up to the time they met Allen, her biracial son. Most white guys I'd heard of, seen, or met were straight-up bigots although they'd bite their own tongues off before admitting it.

I'd also seen how people looked at Danni when we were out with Allen, who despite his brown skin, strongly resembled his mother. When Danni was with Allen, she wasn't white anymore. Many of them looked and treated her with the same contempt that they had for me or Cat.

A fusillade of hard raps sounded at my front door. "That must be Darryl. Maybe he changed his mind," I said.

Cat shook her head. "He's not coming."

I hurried out of the kitchen and faced the worst case scenario. It was Danni's boyfriend, Marcus. He looked freaked out, his eyes wide and agitated.

"I need to talk to you right now," Marcus said to Danni, his voice urgent and high-pitched. "It's about the car."

"What about the car?" she asked. "I know you didn't do anything to my car."

He didn't answer right away.

"Arrrgh," she yelled and ran to my bedroom, slamming the door behind her. I heard my lock click.

Marcus followed her, banging on the door, then shaking the doorknob. "C'mon, woman, we're going home," he said.

"What did you do to Danni's car?" I asked.

"I didn't do anything to it. It was impounded."

"Get your ass on then, and let's go and get it," Cat said.

"You can't."

"Why the fuck not?" Cat demanded.

"You better have a good reason why we can't take the registration, pay the fine, and get Danni's car," I said. This piece of man was a joke.

"They're holding it for evidence," Marcus said, his voice so low I had to strain to hear.

"What did you do, boy?" Cat snapped.

"I didn't do a damn thing. And don't call me boy, bitch—"

"What happened?" Intervention was needed and quickly before Cat went off on Marcus calling her a bitch, sending the situation from bad to worse.

"This chick needed to use it and she got busted . . ." Marcus said.

A collective groan went up.

"You let some other chickenhead skank take Danni's car?" I couldn't believe it.

"I bet he was fucking her too," Winston added helpfully.

"What is she charged with?" Jake cut in.

"Possession and—" Marcus paused. "Here's the deal," he said. "Shellay was turning a trick, and this peckerwood, some fat cat white dude got offed right there inside the car. This nigger just ran up and capped him, so Danni ain't getting that car back anytime soon."

"You sorry son of a bitch!" Cat said, looking around as if she wanted to put her hands on something to cut Marcus. Oh, Lawd.

"Get out," Jake said to Marcus, his voice quiet, but seeming to echo through the room.

My knees weakened in relief because I really didn't want a bad rep with the neighbors over the police coming out to my apartment on a Saturday night.

"Who the fuck are you?" Marcus said, looking Jake up and down.

"It doesn't matter who I am. Get out." There was an under-

29

current of danger in Jake's voice that turned me on even more, if such a thing is possible.

Then Danni opened the bedroom door and ran into the living room. "It's okay, Marcus, I'll go with you."

I rolled my eyes and protest broke out, everybody talking at once.

"No, you're not," Jake said. "I told him to get out and that's what he's going to do."

CHAPTER 4

I sleep, but my heart waketh . . .
—Song of Songs, 5:2

Jake stared at Marcus, his eyes narrowed, glinting green fire. Marcus's nostrils flared. Then, suddenly his eyes widened and he gasped. He looked panicked and fled out my front door, but not before I saw something that flabbergasted me.

Marcus had gotten an erection. Jake turned him on even though I thought Marcus was straight, a regular pussy-hound if there ever was one, to hear Danni tell it.

So even men weren't immune to Jake? I sank into a chair, shaking inside.

Danni pulled out two slices of pizza, stacked them one on top of another and took a huge bite.

"You're eating now? Your car is gone and you have to put that sorry n—" Cat glanced at Jake. "That sorry man out of your apartment!"

"He has a key. What can I do?" she answered.

I picked up a phone book. "I'm calling a twenty-four-hour locksmith. I'll spot you the cash. You're spending the night here tonight and tomorrow we'll pack up his stuff and put it out."

Jake shook his head. "What if he's up at her place when the locksmith arrives? Somebody needs to stay up there until the locks are in place." He looked at one of the pizzas. "Can I take one of these with me?"

"Sure," I said.

"I'll go with you!" Winston said, beaming.

"No, that's all right," Jake said.

"But—" Winston started to protest.

"I said no," Jake repeated.

"Your key?" he asked Danni.

She dug it out of her pocket and handed it over to him visibly shivering as her fingers touched his. "Number 246," she said.

The keys jingled as he grabbed a six-pack of beer. "What's your phone number?" he asked me. "I'll call you after the locksmith leaves."

I went to my desk, pulled out one of my personal cards and handed it to him.

"I'm sorry how Marcus acted. He ruined your party, Luby," Danni said.

"You're not responsible for what Marcus does." I told her and the next instant wished my voice had been less sharp.

"My apartment is a mess," she continued. "My son—" Jake walked out the door in the middle of the sentence with a pizza and beer in hand, and her words trailed away.

Over all, I don't think the evening was a hit.

Afterwards, the three of us sat around overeating pizza, drinking too much beer and staring at junk reality television. Cat got up off the couch, turned off the television and announced, "Let's talk."

Nobody protested that she turned off the TV, but nobody

stopped chewing their pizza either. "If you want to talk, go to it," I said around a mouthful.

Cat sat on the floor and crossed her legs, shockingly immodest, given her short skirt and thong, but we were all girls (Winston included), so what the hell.

"First, Danni, what did you think of Jake?" she asked.

Danni took a swig of beer. "I think I wanna fuck him. Doesn't everybody?"

We all nodded and Winston raised his fist in solidarity.

"Okay, that's taken care of. We'll just wait for Jake to call you."

"There is the tiny problem that he never asked for my number," Danni said. "He asked for Luby's."

"He needed to call her when the locksmith arrived," Winston said.

Danni shrugged. "He has feet, and it's not like it's far away. A man usually will use some excuse to ask for your number if he's doing it in front of other people."

"Danni, I want you to hook up with him," I said. "You need Marcus out of your life."

"I don't see how one has to do with the other. I don't need a man to be able to give Marcus the kiss-off. Jake's not my type for one, and for the second, a guy like that eats hearts for dinner," Danni said, grabbing another slice of pizza. "I think I'm going to be sick," she said, right after stuffing the entire slice into her mouth.

"She's right, you know," Cat said.

"Yeah, with as much pizza as she's eaten I'm surprised she isn't sick already," I said.

"Not about that, about Jake. I think he's interested in you, Luby. And he's bad, bad news," Cat said.

"Hah. Are you telling me something I don't know? In case

you didn't notice, he's white, and a white man's never given me a second glance in my life."

"I doubt it," Danni said. "You're really cute. I bet some white guys have noticed you, but you didn't notice them. I'm white, and I guarantee that it all works the same, no matter the color."

"Whatever. Jake isn't right for me at all, regardless of race. I don't think he's Christian, and as far as I can tell, he doesn't have a job," I said, meaning every word.

"But you still want to fuck him, don't you?" Danni asked.

I was speechless, but unable to deny the fact. "Do you ever think of anything else?" I finally asked.

"Barely. You need to get off that Buppie high horse of yours. You don't know if he's Christian or not," she answered.

What? I raised an astonished eyebrow in her direction. Danni's reading *me*?

"Even if he's not Christian it doesn't mean he's not spiritual. And did you ever bother to check out his ride? I did." Cat said.

My attention was diverted. "What does he drive?"

"A black Toyota Tundra," Cat said.

"One of those manly trucks," Winston said, obviously thrilled.

"Yep, one of those big-ass expensive pickup trucks, a new Japanese model, no less. He didn't get a ride like that without either serious cash or damn fine credit," Cat said.

"He's got money," Danni said. "I can smell money."

"Honey, if you can smell money, why don't you find a nigga that has some?" Cat asked.

"That's my new project," Danni said in a dry voice. "I'm looking for somebody like your man Darryl."

"If you honestly believe that he has any money, you can have him," Cat said, studying her nails.

"What's up with you and Darryl?" I asked. I could tell that Cat meant her words. Something had been wrong with them for a long while, but I wasn't able to tell exactly what. Besides it was a blessed change of subject.

She shrugged.

We all waited silently for her to continue. My girlfriend sense told me that Cat had more to say, much more.

"When we first got together in high school, there was this hot feeling between us, we were proud of each other and we cared. We never wanted to hurt each other." Cat sighed and drew up her knees. "I don't know when we stopped caring . . . maybe the last four years?"

"If you two love each other, it must be fixable. With effort—" Winston said.

She looked at him. "No. It's not fixable." Her eyes dropped to the floor. "Darryl and I never talked. We mainly looked good together. We're a great-looking couple, you know."

Then I was stunned when I realized that Cat was crying. I got a box of Kleenex and moved on the floor beside her. Danni was already on the other side, her arm around Cat's shoulders. Winston sat on the couch, still, looking extremely uncomfortable.

I'd never seen Cat cry before. She was fearless, strong, and quick-witted, always ready with a snappy comeback. She never let anything get her down.

Watching Cat cry was like watching a panther brought down.

"I gotta go," Winston said right before he scuttled out the door. I looked after him and shook my head. Whether gay or not, feminine tears and angst still rattles a man.

Cat emptied the box of tissues, using one after another. After a while, she blew her nose and composed herself. "I don't like Darryl anymore. I want out. I hate my life," she said.

I know a woman doesn't cry like Cat unless it hurts and hurts bad. "I'm sorry, baby."

She looked away from me, glass-fragile. "When something as

important as your marriage falls apart, there's a sense of failure, you know?"

I didn't know, but both Danni and I nodded.

"Darryl and I really never worked that well once we were away from the high school and college social props. That's the real reason why we've never started a family or really settled down and made a home. He's depressed. He's turned into a different man."

I hated the thought of marriages splitting up, divorce and dissolution, but in the face of Cat's sadness, I couldn't suggest a prop like counseling. "Are you going to file for divorce?" I asked.

Cat reached for the remote and clicked the television on, staring in its direction, morose, but resolute also. "Yeah. I really don't want to talk about it anymore."

Danni got to her feet and started gathering beer bottles and the remains of our pizza.

I went into the bedroom to lie down on my bed, picking up a paperback I had on my bedside table. I heard Danni cleaning the kitchen and Cat was in the closet outside my bedroom probably pulling out linens for the couch.

All in all, for a Saturday night, it was pretty much a bust, but something inside me felt good anyway because I was with my friends.

Cat was long asleep on the couch and I was in my bed beside Danni, listening to her deep regular breathing, when the phone rang. I knocked over a glass of water on the bedside table, trying to get to it.

"Fuck!" I said as I lifted the phone to my ear.

"An interesting way to say hello, but if that's what's on your mind . . ."

The dark velvet of Jake's voice caressed my ear and my toes

involuntarily curled. *Oh, fuck.* I glanced over at Danni, but she was unmoving. She slept like the dead.

"Oh, hi, sorry, I spilled my water—"

"The locksmith just left Danni's apartment," he said. "I'll slide the keys under your door on my way home, okay?"

"Okay."

"Good night, then. See you soon."

I hung up with the words *see you soon*, echoing over and over through my mind and knew I wouldn't get back to sleep for ages.

Sexual awareness zinged through me, like a hot freight train. His voice, his body, his scent. What if he were lying here instead of Danni? What would I do? How would he touch me?

My hand crept between my thighs before I was aware of Danni's sleeping form. I rose from the bed as quietly as I could, and went to the bathroom.

I visualized the hard rush of water from the hand-held shower-head as if Jake's fingers played on my clit and moments later an orgasm thundered through me.

Mere, empty, physical satisfaction. Humans have to have it, but without another's touch it was hollow.

I dried quickly and picked my gown up from the floor. When I returned to bed, I soon drifted off to sleep.

My arms hugged a plant I picked up on clearance over at my favorite florist cum horticulturist over on the Plaza. Jake sat on the bench out front with one of his big old books propped open on his knees.

As soon as he saw me, he closed the book, tucked it under his arm and stood. "Need some help?" he asked, reaching for the plant. I almost dropped it when I realized that as soon as he'd drawn close to me, the feeling was back, a heightened sexual

37

awareness roaring through me. It wasn't a fluke. I still hoped that maybe it was a PMS side effect brought on by the time of the month nearing. But this was crazy. "Thanks," I said, not knowing if I could bear being close to him in the elevator.

I wanted to suggest that we take the stairs, but it was crazy to expect him to climb five floors with an armful of plant.

We rode up silently. I did my best to try to hold my breath. He stood aside to let me lead the way. In front of my door, as I fumbled with my purse and keys awkwardly, he put the plant on the floor and took the keys out of my hands. He touched my hands in the process and it affected me so much I almost gasped.

"Where do you want this?"

"Set it down anywhere," I said, breathing hard. He bent over and set it carefully in a corner. Beautiful.

Every cell in my body screamed for satisfaction. I waded through a haze of lust. Dust motes froze in the air, and I knew I couldn't take another breath until I touched him. Is this how men felt? Why weren't they all mad? I couldn't stand it another moment. So as soon as he straightened, I walked into his arms.

CHAPTER 5

. . . for thy love is better than wine.
—Song of Songs, 1:2

He embraced me without hesitation and I closed my eyes in thankfulness. He pulled me close, his hands dropping to my rear in an intimate caress. I raised my face to his and met his kiss.

Sweet Jesus. I gave it up without a second's hesitation, all restraint abandoned and delirious with hunger.

Jake's kiss was tender and hungry and hot and I wanted to devour him whole. He tasted of honey, cinnamon and smoke. His tongue teased the cavern of my mouth tasting me in turn, his breath growing harsh and hard as his body.

I molded to the length of him, rubbing against his hard length in wanton need, my legs spreading. I pulled him toward my bedroom, tugging at his jeans. "I need it now." I kicked off my shoes and dropped my suit jacket to the floor.

His eyes burned my body, hot, eager and caressing.

"I know," he said. "And I'm going to give it to you." He licked his lips and his hand dropped below his waist and grasped his generous bulge. He wanted to see my body. I could tell as if he had whispered the words in my ears.

I unzipped my skirt at the back, and slowly wriggled out of it to the sensuous beat of my heart. I kicked it to the side then peeled off my panty hose. I heard him murmur in approval.

I stood before him in panties and bra, unashamed, with my arms open, beckoning and pleading, my hips writhing to that inner beat. The sex was winding within me, hot and sinuous, like a snake that would burst through my skin unless soon released.

He growled, an alien sound, a dangerous predator, but I was unafraid. I offered myself to him, without reservation, for him to work his will.

"You're beautiful," he said, his eyes playing over my bare skin.

I didn't see him move toward me, but I was in his arms, his hands at my back unsnapping my bra. My breasts sprang free, full and brown and he groaned as he buried his face in them.

I moaned in turn and he teased one nipple then the other with his tongue, twirling and suckling, the sensation pulling juices from deep within me.

Then he pulled my hips to him and his fingers probed my dripping pussy, expertly rotating around my clit. Near sobbing with need, "Now," I gasped. "Please, God, now."

"Yes," he said, his breath hissing through his teeth. He withdrew his fingers from inside me and my knees almost buckled. He moved me toward the bed and laid me gently down, like a precious object.

He pulled the T-shirt over his head and pulled his wallet out of his back pocket and removed a condom. "After this we'll be able to talk, and I'd really like to talk to you."

I heard the words, but didn't really understand them. My need had devoured all the empty spaces and words were meaningless. He dropped his jeans to the floor and stood in front of me, naked, fully erect. He unrolled the condom over his erection, not taking his eyes off me. Beautiful. I cared about nothing but him inside me.

We were on the bed then, his lips tasting me and his hands learning every inch of my skin. He pulled off the soaked panties, far too slowly, and his head started to dip to my rotating, urgent hips.

"I need you inside me," I said. I would go mad if he didn't bury himself inside me. He covered me, my legs immediately opening to engulf his big, hard cock.

My hands ran frantically over the smooth skin of his back.

"Fuck me," I begged. He obliged and plunged into me with a deep stroke. I was so wet, he felt like a churn making sweet butter. I'd never felt anything like it before. My breath caught in my throat.

"You're so tight," he said with a groan.

I couldn't have said anything if I tried. My pussy worked around his shaft, squeezing and rotating as he plunged in and out with a grind against my clit on the downstroke. Every fiber of my body soaked him in and my world narrowed to every ridge of his shaft and the head of his big dick as it moved against my walls with sweet, liquid friction. I was expanding from my center out, riding on a bubble of ecstasy.

He kissed me hard and plunged his tongue in deep, in time with his dick. He pulled out almost to the tip and then plunged in deep, hard and wet, making me scream for the first time in my life. I wanted to inhale him into myself.

Then he broke and bucked like a stallion gone wild and I went with him, giving it back to him and more. We shook the bed, urgent and frantic, nothing existing but the feel of his dick inside me, and the fire of my pussy.

I felt his hoarse growl against my neck. I'd expanded like a balloon pumped too full in the split second before it burst. He held me in a space where everything stilled for what felt like an eternity. I felt as if I had died.

And then the feeling came crashing, obliterating me with a shuddering beginning to a sensation of pleasure so exquisite it almost cut me, tearing through me in shattering waves until it finally subsided, and I was back to myself.

I opened my eyes to his quaking shudders. He relaxed in my arms, drained.

I was drained too, too fatigued to move, too tired to breathe deep, limp.

After a time, I lifted my head. "Do you want a beer?" I asked him. I knew I needed one, my mouth was parched, my body felt as dry as autumn leaves.

I grabbed my robe from the hook on the door and went to the bathroom, washed up and used the toilet. I looked at my face in the mirror, hesitant, as if I expected to see another person reflected there.

It was the same face that always stared back at me, albeit with mussed make-up, tossed hair, and kiss-bruised lips.

I went to the kitchen and stood in front of the refrigerator, letting my robe fall open and the cool air bathe my heated body. I took out two Heinekens and opened them. I was sore between my legs, something I'd never experienced.

The entire experience was new, from my mindless passion at the beginning to the incredible ending.

My few previous lovers were completely wanting in comparison. I felt regret for what I'd missed all these years. I took a sip of beer and felt the cool, slightly bitter liquid travel down my throat. Was I going to be a white man's whore now? I certainly had acted like one. Jake was as addictive as I imagined crack to be.

I slowly walked back to the bedroom. What did Jake really think of me? This was way beyond screwing on the first date—more like screwing on the first hello.

He had propped himself against the headboard of my seven-foot-four poster bed, and grinned in appreciation as I handed him a beer. I never had a man under my canopy before. I was embarrassed by the decoration of my bedroom—black, raspberry pink, and bright blue, gauzy floaty fabrics and silk. Cat always teased me about decorating my bedroom as if it was in a bordello.

I placed the beer on the beside table and moved to lie beside Jake. He pulled me to him and pushed my hair back and kissed my ear. "Lose the robe," he said. "I like to look at your body."

Heat flushed my face. My former wanton lust had disappeared and I didn't quite know what to do with this white man in my bed, whom I barely knew. He was an extremely handsome white man, but it still didn't change the basic facts. Guilt stabbed at me. I'd been mindless, crazed with lust.

He regarded me. "It's not your fault. And it wasn't all me, either. I let it happen because I liked you and wanted to talk to you, and I'm a little lonely."

My jaw tightened at the insult. "Thanks a lot," I said, sarcasm laced in the three words.

He sighed. "I didn't mean it like that. What I meant is that I can't really be around people unless we . . ." Now he looked embarrassed.

"You're telling me you refuse to have anything to do with a person unless you sleep with them first." I slid out of bed. "That's a good one."

"I'm saying that the person can have nothing to do with me. You know how it was between us. You could barely stop yourself from reaching out to touch me whenever you were near me. I bet it's that way with every one of your friends too. People don't interact with me. They're too busy lusting for me."

My eyes narrowed. "More than a little egotistical, hmmm?" I got up to pull a pair of panties out of my drawer.

"Ego has nothing to do with it, and you know it. It's more like my own personal curse. I don't feel like a man half the time. I feel like a walking dildo. It's as if I have to get past the sex to even have a decent conversation." He passed a darting glance at me. "I don't choose to have sex with just anybody."

He was telling me that I was special. Mollified, I remembered how Danni, Cat, and I talked after he'd left about how fine he was and what we'd like to do to him. Winston begged me to tell him if Jake was gay, and was ecstatic when I said I didn't know.

"You're an attractive man. A lot of people would be happy to have your particular curse."

"Believe me, they wouldn't." He raised his head and met my eyes. The loneliness there rocked me. "Please come back beside me."

I was powerless to refuse him. I dropped the robe and slid under the cool satin sheets.

"You really believe you're cursed?" I asked.

He nodded, his beautiful green eyes sad. "I know it."

"My mother is crazy," I blurted out. "My grandmother told me my mother hears voices of the dead and wasn't strong enough to deal with it."

He didn't say anything, but took my hand in his large one and played with my fingers.

"That happens sometimes," he murmured.

I wanted to ask which one, hearing the voices of the dead or going crazy? But I didn't say anything because I was suspecting he was too intimately acquainted with crazy.

"I don't do this all the time," I said instead. "Although by the décor, it may look it." I glanced around, embarrassed.

"I like it. And I know you don't do this often." He smiled a little wicked grin. "Neither do I."

I grinned back at him, "No way do I believe that."

"Okay, only with select people I like very much."

"How do you know me well enough to decide how much you like me? I could be terrible. In fact, I probably am."

"I could see who you were the moment I first laid eyes on you." He touched my cheek lightly. "And I liked what I saw."

"I couldn't think about anything but getting your jeans off you."

He withdrew his hand and laced his fingers behind his head. "I know. But it'll be better now. Can we be friends?"

I caught my breath. Then I realized that he'd said absolutely the right thing. We didn't really know each other. He'd made no promises to call me, no lies or evasion, but only a simple request for friendship. For now, it was perfect.

I smiled at him. "Yes, we can be friends."

He exhaled with something that looked suspiciously like relief. "Good."

"You realize that we planned to set you up with Danni."

"I figured."

A bolt flew through me out of nowhere, and it took me a moment to identify the emotion. It was jealousy. I bit my lip. Jealousy was ugly and cold, an emotion I was totally unused to. Resentment for Danni filled me. She was right for him with her white skin, colorless hair, and limpid blue eyes. Everybody wanted Danni. And she said she wanted to fuck Jake.

"Are you going to sleep with her too?" I asked, my voice raw.

He took too long to answer. I withdrew my hand and stuck it under the covers.

"No. She's pretty, but she doesn't appeal to me," he said.

"Why not?" I asked. "Most men seem to like her better than me."

"Most men are idiots."

I couldn't argue with that. I relaxed slowly, ashamed of my base emotion.

"She's confused and very hurt. She's lost her way. I hope she finds it."

My mouth fell open a bit at his presumptuousness.

"She's lost in a different way than you are," he added.

"What makes you think I'm lost?" I asked, somewhat defensive.

"You don't have what you want, and don't know how to find it."

I was speechless, his assessment was too accurate.

"Do you know what I want?" I finally asked.

That sexy, slow smile spread over his face. "No. But you don't know either."

I shook my head and took the bottle back and tipped it. I was starving. "What do you plan to do for dinner?"

"Take you out on our first date. That is, if we can shower together."

"Why? You don't like to shower alone?"

"When you're around, I don't."

Jake washed me, moving the soothing soap in between my legs until I moaned with pleasure. "You realize I'm going to have to rinse well," he said, taking the showerhead down and turning the massage dial. He pulled me to him. His erection was solid against my side and he rolled my nipple between his fingers.

Then he directed the stream of warm water between my legs, directly on my clit.

I gasped and sagged against him, the pressure against my clit intense and unrelenting.

He supported me against his legs and used his other hand to reach down and slide between my legs, his aim unwavering with the shower jet. He moved two fingers into my vagina, rotating and massaging it at a particular spot.

I screamed as the orgasm crashed and took me like a wave once smashed me down to the ocean floor and tumbled me in the sand and water.

After a last shuddering breath, I lowered myself to my knees, the water cascading over my face and hair and closed my lips around his member.

It was something I'd never done before, but I needed to at that moment, very badly. My hand barely went around it. I knew to be careful with my teeth and swirled my tongue around the head and its ridge. It was Jake's turn to gasp as his hand tightened in my hair. I enclosed his penis in my mouth and sucked, my tongue hitting the spots that made his hands tense and grip my hair.

It wasn't long before he stiffened with a groan and pulled out of my mouth, his ejaculate hitting my breasts and sliding down the drain. We leaned together, our breaths sliding down our skin.

"That friend thing?" I asked.

"Mmmmmmmm?"

"Do friends and hot sex go together?"

"Sure . . . but, very carefully," he replied.

When we dressed to go out, Jake talked me into leaving my hair alone and I felt self-conscious. I never got it wet in the shower. I don't know what I was thinking. It kinked up nearly instantly and I had a fit, but he was enchanted.

"You look like a singer. Sexy and exotic. Leave your hair be and don't cover it," he said.

I must have lost my mind and did what he said. The result was akin to a giant afro. I coiled my fingers through my hair to make it lay down.

"Where do you want to eat?" he asked.

"Beanie's," I immediately said and gave him directions.

A short time later, we were sitting at Beanie's in a corner booth. I don't know what made me suggest a soul food restaurant on our first date. I guess I wanted to see how he would deal with it. Besides, I couldn't think of anything I wanted to eat more than greens and cornbread, and you don't get that at McDonalds.

So far he'd handled it well, ordering sweet tea and ribs with all the right fixin's, and not seeming uncomfortable in the slightest.

I was surprised that nobody gave my head a second glance. But when I looked around, I realized that there were all sorts of hair, straightened, sure, but also locks, braids, and hair flowing in a natural texture like my own. How had I missed the revolution and stayed addicted to the hot comb?

"So what is with all the books on magic and sorcery?" I asked him, a little nervous. I really wanted to ask him if he'd ever dated a sister before, but couldn't quite get that question out.

He played with the silverware. "I'm studying them," he said.

"You want to be a sorcerer? You believe in it?"

"I don't want to be a sorcerer. I'm looking for the solution to a problem I have."

"You think magic can solve problems?"

"It can solve my problems."

I lowered my eyes to my tea, not wanting them to betray my feelings. I knew that anybody that good in bed who seemed so sweet had to be too good to be true. I wasn't afraid of this man I hardly knew though, not a bit.

"Most people don't believe in magic, Jake."

He shrugged. "Most people are blind."

The waitress was standing at our table again, her eyes fixed on Jake. We both looked at her, inquiring, because there was no food in her hands.

"Um, I wanted to see if you wanted any appetizers. Some more drinks?"

She'd just refilled our drinks two minutes ago. My eyes narrowed as she stared at Jake and licked her lips. I knew exactly what she was feeling and I didn't like it.

"We don't need anything until we get our food. And I doubt we'll need anything after that," I said.

She had the nerve to roll her eyes at me and switched away. I hated it that this woman was going to be bringing me my food.

"That's why I don't go out much," Jake said in a low voice.

I chewed on my lower lip. I had to admit that it was weird that every blessed person who came near him seemed to want to have sex with him. I glanced around and sure enough, the women at the tables around us could hardly keep their eyes off him.

He was good-looking and all, but this was plain weird. I knew that black women tended to ignore white men. They'd always barely registered as sexual objects to me, because they weren't possibilities. They weren't interested in me because of my skin color. I was used to being invisible to white men. They rarely saw me, whereas a black man would immediately assess my face and figure as an attractive, desirable woman.

So all these black women tripping over a white man, no matter how fine, was freaky. No way was it natural.

"I told you," he said.

I hated the way I felt as if he could read my mind. "It's like this all the time for you?" I asked. "People hitting on you wherever you go?"

"Yes, uh well, until I have sex with them." He grinned at me. "Now that we've got that out of the way, we can be friends."

Got that out of the way? I looked away to hide my expression.

I watched the waitress pick up the plates until she headed to us. I wanted to make sure my plate made no detours.

She dropped my plate on the table and hovered over Jake. "We're fine here," he said. "Thanks," dismissing her.

She gave him another bat of her eyes before switching her ample rear away.

My appetite was gone. I watched Jake dig into his ribs while I toyed with my greens.

"What's wrong?" he asked, once he looked up from his plate.

"What if it's true? That anybody who comes close is inexplicably attracted to you? What would a person do?"

"After a while they would be desperate to be free and live a normal life and . . . to have friends and people who they knew truly cared about him." His voice had lowered to a whisper.

"What about family?"

He took a swig of tea. "They're unaffected."

"Jake . . . don't take this wrong, but what makes you think you're cursed rather than something else weird going on? There are lots of weird things in the world."

"I agree."

"It could be a genetic anomaly, some freak pheromone thing."

"I guess it could be what you could call—a genetic anomaly."

He smiled at me, his teeth so white, I blinked.

"See?" I said, with some relief. He was great in bed and seemed like a nice guy, but I was getting tired of dealing with the weird stuff.

We ate in silence, and I observed the reaction of the women around him. It didn't let up. More women brushed by our table on the way to the bathroom than were reasonable.

"How can you tell which people are being real or not?" I asked, unable to let the topic go as I dearly wanted to do.

He lay down the rib and picked up a napkin and wiped his hands. "It's never real. Would you have jumped in my arms otherwise? Be honest."

I swallowed. In my entire life, I'd never done more than glance at an attractive white man, and that usually in a photo, a movie, or a video. I'd also never been so sexually uninhibited in my life with anyone. In the future, I doubt that jumping in bed with men after the first hi would be conducive to my overall self-esteem.

I shook my head no. "But what's done is done," I said.

"Always," he said. A hint of his sexy crooked grin played over his face before he tipped his glass. I shivered when I realized that maybe it wouldn't be easy to let the weirdness go.

The next day, I cooked for Jake. This was the equivalent of giving up my virginity, me cooking for a man. I hoped he appreciated it.

I surveyed my roast chicken, new potatoes, green beans, and corn. It looked edible, which was an extra bonus. I was going to make hot dogs and popcorn, but decided that the fabulous loving he laid on me the day before was worth more effort.

Jake dropped a kiss on my lips when I opened the door. A possessive boyfriend sort of kiss, not a friend kiss at all.

"I hope you're hungry," I said.

"Starving."

"Let's eat then." I steered him to my feast set out on the dining room table.

He ate as if he hadn't had a square meal in a week, and looked at me with a crooked smile of appreciation on his lips. "You are very special, do you know that?" He reached out and touched my cheek. It was as if his fingers were live wires, his touch was that potent.

That's when I got the inkling that this whole relationship was going to screw with my head. I admit it, I panicked. "I think I should run a personal ad online," I said.

Then I realized that it wasn't a bad idea. My newfound sexual exuberance must mean I need a man way more than I thought I did, and to me a man meant eventual commitment—something Jake would never offer.

He lifted his brow. "Why?"

"To meet men."

"My question was why do you want to meet men when you have one already?"

"Do I? You said we were friends. Friendship does not a man-woman relationship make."

"I doubt most friends are as intimate," he said.

"That's it, Jake. We're not really friends, not really anything but sexual partners, and that isn't me."

He touched my face, making my heart pound as if it were careening out of control. Unfair tactics.

"I don't want to be hurt," I said softly.

"Am I what you really want in a man?" he asked. "Do you honestly see yourself loving me? Making a home with me? As anything else but your boy toy? Your sex stud?" He dropped his hand leaving me feeling bereft. "Here's a newsflash, baby. I don't want to be hurt either, but it goes with the territory."

"That's crazy, Jake. You're the most desirable man I've ever met."

"I'm the most desirable man anyone has ever met. That's what makes it meaningless."

I bit my lip, wanting to go ahead and give my all to him, but my instinct for self-preservation was strong. "After we made love the first time, you asked if we could be friends. So let's do it. Let's be friends. I need to leave the sex alone for awhile and clear my head. I can barely think when you make love to me."

His face looked stiff and unyielding.

"I want to be your friend. Please, Jake."

"It sounds as if you want to see other men. That's what I can't understand."

"I need to do this, Jake. If we're right, other men won't matter."

He shook, putting me in mind of a large dog.

"I won't sleep with anybody without first letting you know I'm starting that sort of relationship if . . ." My voice trailed away, unsure, but needing to ask him.

He turned and looked at me.

"If you'll promise to let me know the same," I said.

The thought of Jake making love to another woman cut sharp. But the pain would fade after I recovered from what his lovemaking did to me. "You're like an addictive drug," I said. "One good hit can make you go crazy. It's killing me inside."

He stood from the table and sighed. "I probably understand better than you can guess."

He moved to the living room, and crouched on the floor by my stereo, going through my CDs. "You know what? Our taste in music isn't all that different."

My musical taste doesn't run to strictly radio top forty R&B and hip-hop, but I don't think it's that strange for a black chick. I like good soul vocalists, Nina Simone, Aretha Franklin, some mellow jazz, some acid jazz, some classic old school and Motown, some funk, along with lots of blues. I loved the blues—especially electric blues.

It floored me that Jake would consider my musical tastes were anything close to a white guy's. I assumed that the white guys who didn't listen to country, listened to screechy rock music of various sorts. I don't think I had a single rock CD.

"You don't like rock?" I asked.

"I like some of it. It looks like you do too."

"I don't have any rock."

"What do you call all these Janis Joplin CDs? You have everything of hers, Stevie Ray Vaughn, Eric Clapton . . ."

"I call that the blues."

He chuckled. "Semantics. Hey, let's go to the Robert Cray concert." He looked at his watch. "We have an hour."

"It's been sold out for weeks."

"We'll get tickets from the scalpers," he said, rubbing his fingers in the universal sign for money.

"That'll cost a fortune."

He stood and slapped my rear lightly. "I'm buying. Let's go."

I didn't count on the huge wad of cash Jake wielded. We got primo seats.

After the concert, we went to Starbucks at the Plaza near our apartment building. I was happily sipping my venti sugar-free vanilla soy latte when Jake gave me a look. I knew exactly what that look meant, and couldn't prevent a flush of sexual awareness.

The *look* wasn't a friend thing. I frowned at him. It was hard enough to try not to fall into girlfriend mode with all the curious and envious glances others cast my way because I was with major gorgeous guy, in addition to the interracial aspect, without him giving me the *look*.

"What time do you have to be at work tomorrow?" he asked.

"It's pretty flexible. I do have a lot of briefs I need to finish up."

"What sort of lawyer are you?"

"Our firm handles mainly corporate law. I don't have any cases. I'm only a junior associate. I assist the partners."

"Do you like your job?"

I thought about it. I'd been at the firm a year and a half. My job was hardly challenging. They never gave me anything hard to do. I graduated top of my class from an Ivy League school, so I doubted that I was incompetent and I knew I wasn't dumb. But I'd never been assigned to do anything that would challenge me and showcase my stuff. I knew better than to take the initiative because I'd tried that once and got slapped down like a bothersome gnat.

My job was easy, paid relatively well, and was secure not only because I made no waves, but because I was the only African American woman in the office, and they killed two affirmative action birds with one stone. Heaven knew they didn't want to have to hire another one of us.

"No," I said. "I don't like my job."

I ran my finger around the rim of my cup. "What do you do, Jake?" I'd been dying to ask that question for a while, but when I had the opportunity I always seemed to forget.

"Right now, I'm studying my books. I bought a desk and computer for Internet research yesterday."

"Oh. So you're independently wealthy?" My tone was a tad sarcastic and I could have clapped my hands over my mouth as soon as the question slipped out.

"Back home, I worked as a veterinarian. But I suppose you'd consider my family well-off, yes."

He considered me with those piercing green eyes.

I closed my mouth because my jaw was hanging open. I had to recover from the fact that the most gorgeous guy I'd ever seen seemed to be quite attracted to me, was the stone-cold shit in bed, and was not only *well-off*, but apparently also had a graduate degree. Good Lord.

"I'm going to get another coffee. Would you like something else?" I asked.

"I'm fine." He leaned back in his chair.

I returned with another one of the mochas he'd ordered because I'd remembered he said he didn't want anything only after I paid the cashier. I guess I don't handle being flabbergasted that well.

I put both of the coffees in front of me and sat down.

"You must be very thirsty."

I heard the hint of laughter under his tone. "Don't you dare laugh."

"Never. He reached and took the extra coffee, not taking his eyes off me.

I squirmed under his regard. "Why are you watching me?"

"You're a beautiful woman. More so than any I've seen in a long time."

My face heated. "Have you dated a lot of black women?" I asked him politely.

"I haven't dated any. Except you, of course. There aren't many blacks in Montana or in North Dakota, where I went to school."

I guess not. I was disappointed, mainly because I don't particularly like being the first black anything.

"That you don't recognize your own beauty is a testament to the ignorance of those around you," he said. "Your features and body are perfect."

Perfect? I barely controlled myself from snorting in my coffee. "I'm too dark-skinned even for some of the brothers. When I'm out with Cat, they almost run over me to get to her."

"You're prettier than Cat."

I looked at him. He was being truthful. I liked the way I looked well enough, and knew I was attractive, but as a brown-skinned woman with soft features rather than chiseled European ones, I had never considered myself a beauty.

I appreciated my small, voluptuous but firm figure, but I never dressed to show it off and dreaded the inevitable day when gravity would drift everything southward.

"I think I know what makes you more special," he said.

More compliments? The man was going to cause me to fall over in a faint if he didn't quit.

"You don't have the self-awareness beautiful women have. You disregard how you look."

"Do you disregard how you look too?" I asked him. He had to know he was a beautiful man. There was nothing feminine about his features, but everywhere we went, women (and some men) stared at him.

He inclined his head once. He knew. But I sensed that it brought him no pleasure at all.

I looked over at the table next to us where three women sat, barely able to pretend they were drinking their coffee because so much of their attention was concentrated on us. "I wonder why he's with *her?*" one of them said loudly after they'd seen me glance their way.

Jake turned his head and surveyed them. They seemed to hold their breath under his gaze. "Because she's far superior to any of you," he said. "Let's go," he told me.

Oh, *snap.* I looked back as I followed him out of the coffee shop. Bitches were floored.

Back at our apartment building, he walked me to my door. He started to turn to me, and then he caught himself. I knew he'd meant to kiss me, but realized in time that kissing didn't go with the friend thing. It took every bit of willpower that I could muster to turn the key in the door and say goodbye instead of forget the friend thing as I dragged him to my bed.

But I didn't. I closed the door behind me, leaning against it, listening to his steps recede, tingling with this weird excitement. It took me a while to identify it, but eventually I did. *Oh no.* Fuck, I was falling in love.

Jake was like a drug or too much liquor. Like Cat would say, I was getting addicted to the dick. I had to explore my options. I needed to get out, to give myself a change with other men. Men who wanted to be more than friends.

Suitable men. Professional, black Christian men. Cat said that the only way I was going to find a "black church-going nerd sitting at home alone in front of his computer, the mouse glued to his right hand" was to run an ad.

I booted up my computer, got out my credit card, and logged on.

CHAPTER 6

I opened to my beloved . . .
—Song of Songs, 5:6

I'd just gotten in from work and kicked my shoes off when the phone rang. When I picked up the phone and heard Jake's voice, an involuntary grin spread over my face.

"What are you doing for dinner?" Jake asked.

"Eating, I hope."

"Want to go out? Or I can cook," he said.

I sank on my couch. "You can cook?" I squeaked. Lord, was the man perfect or what?

"I can," he said. "And would you care to sample my delicacies?"

I almost choked. Resisting this man's delicacies was damn near impossible.

"What time?" I asked.

"Give me a couple of hours. Guess what? I bought furniture."

"Wow," I said, easing off my shoes. An excited fluttery feeling filled my chest. I hadn't had that feeling since I was fifteen and had a huge crush on this boy who eventually asked me out. Oh, no.

"I bought a real bed," he continued, making my stomach dip

59

as images flashed through my mind on the two of us on that bed. "And a dining table, and a living room set."

"Big spender," I murmured.

"You're worth every penny."

My mouth dried. This was lover's banter, not friend's casual conversation. I had to face the fact that I'd tripped over Jake's dreamy green eyes, shaggy dark brown hair, golden skin, and big, giant—

"Why don't you come over around eight?" he was asking.

"That sounds good. Do you want me to bring something?"

"Just yourself."

My eyes closed as I murmured assent. I was lost to this man's loving and most of all, his sweetness. I unwound the scarf from around my neck. "I can't wait," I whispered.

"Neither can I," he whispered back.

A few beats went by, punctuated by only our breathing. Beats full of mutual longing and desire.

"See you then," I said and hung up the phone.

This was it. I'd finally met a man I could love and who was white and I didn't know shit about him other than that he was kind, hot as hell, and seemed to be utterly turned on by me. I didn't want to be like most of the people who I went to school and worked with and deny my inner racism. I didn't have that luxury.

I needed to face my beliefs that were hanging me up regarding Jake. I felt that white guys fucked us occasionally, but rarely had relationships or married us. Down deep, I felt he'd never really value me as much as he would if my skin were light and pinkish. My ego and my pride couldn't take being a white man's whore for too long.

I went to the bathroom, and peered at my bruised neck in the mirror. His passionate kisses on my neck during our frenzied

lovemaking had left dark bruises against my brown skin that I
had had to cover for work. I'd mention it to him tonight. We
needed to have another talk. The friend thing wasn't working
out. The lover thing might never work out. My emotions were
on the line and, unlike my body, I couldn't afford to fuck with
those.

I went home and sat down at my desk. I pulled open a drawer
and took out a piece of paper with my personal ad on it. I read
it over again. It seemed right, but I wasn't sure. I had a lot riding
on this.

I picked up the phone and dialed Danni. I got her answering
machine and left a message. "I have something I want you to
look at. Can you come up to my place when you get in? Bring
Allen."

Then I rang Cat, no answer. Then I remembered that today
Darryl was at the station. I rang Cat's cell. "You busy? Can you
come by?"

"Not really, I'm out shopping. You got anything to eat?" she
asked.

"Whatever you can find in the freezer."

I heard Cat chuckle. "It figures. Slide one of those dinners in
the microwave for me."

A half hour later, Cat polished off the small microwave dinner and listened to me read my personal ad. "This isn't like you
at all," she said.

"The Lord helps those who help themselves, and I have come
to the conclusion that I need a man in my life."

Cat frowned. "You told me the other day that you and Jake
nearly fucked the sheets off the bed."

"I didn't put it like that."

"That's what you meant."

I couldn't deny that. "Cat, Jake said he only wants to be my friend."

"Ohhhhh, he wants to be free to fuck other people?"

"No! And would you stop using that word? It's giving me a headache."

"Negro, pleeeze. You use it all the time."

"Never mind," I said. "Geez."

"Anyway, you told me you saw each other yesterday and you've made plans for the weekend together, and he wants to fuck other people? That's bullshit. It's not like you fu—uh, *went to bed* with him once and he never called after that."

"I don't think he wants to sleep with other people. But even if I disregard the tiny matter of the friend thing, I can't get around that he's not for me. He's not Christian for chrissakes." I shredded a napkin to bits.

"Oh, he's Jewish?"

"No, he's not Jewish. I don't know what he is. He studies sorcery."

"What? Is that like a Quaker?"

"It's like a magician."

"Oh, sorcery. I didn't hear you right." Cat laid her fork down in the empty plastic tray and regarded me. "Is it the David Copperfield or Houdini kind, or the sort where you have to sacrifice chickens to Satan and shit like that?"

"I think the chicken sort."

"Sheeeit."

That meant that Cat was near speechless and it took a lot to render Cat speechless. "Even if I disregarded that, he'd still never believe I love him or love me back because he thinks he's under some magic curse that makes everybody irresistibly sexually attracted to him."

Cat picked up her can of Diet Pepsi. "Nuts, huh? That's too

bad." Then she perked up. "But there's plenty of medication nowadays that works wonders—"

"Cat!"

"Okay, okay. I get it now." Her face fell. "I was really hoping that you'd stepped out."

"With my mother, you know I don't deal well with crazy. You know what Grandma told me?"

"Nope, what?"

"That I'm in danger of losing my marbles too when I turn twenty-seven. Worse, she's apparently lost some marbles already. She told me that she sees the future and my mother hears the voices of dead people."

"Like that boy in *Sixth Sense?*"

"No, he saw dead people."

"Is your grandmother doing all right otherwise? No change in her ability to do stuff?"

"Not that I can tell and I've been looking."

"She may not be all that crazy then. Maybe she's right. You hear about that shit all the time." Cat lowered her voice. "Don't tell anybody, but I went to a psychic once."

I lifted my eyebrows. "You paid money? Was it worth it?"

"Every penny. This chick at work turned me on to it. That psychic knew some stuff about me that nobody could possibly know and she told me not to marry Darryl. Dammit to hell that I didn't pay any attention to her."

"I guess I gotta wait and see what happens on my twenty-seventh birthday. Maybe I'll grow horns."

There was a knock at the door. "It's me and Allen," Danni called. "Let me in."

"Hey, Aunt Luby," Allen said as soon as I opened the door. "Can I go into your room and watch MudDog Rangers? Mom said I could if I asked."

I grinned at him and ruffled his mop of burnished brown curls. "Want some milk and cookies?"

"Sure!" he said.

"No, you don't. You just were out and had a huge dinner. You can have something later," Danni said.

"Sorry," I said to her after Allen had left the room and loud noises were emanating from the television in my bedroom.

"That's all right, but he cleaned his plate and had chocolate cake and ice cream for dessert. I swear, I don't know where he puts it. What have you been up to, stranger? We haven't seen hide nor hair of you," Danni said.

I'd been dreading this moment. But Danni was my girl, I had to lay it out for her. "I've been seeing Jake," I said.

Cat chuckled as she returned from the kitchen and set her stack of chocolate chip cookies and large glass of milk on the coffee table.

"You lucky bitch," Danni said. She sat in a chair and tucked her feet under her. "Now, give us all the details on that luscious race-mixing jungle bunny lovin' you got going on."

I grinned. She was taking my copping her stud-to-be rather well. "Who's a jungle bunny?" I asked, mock-outraged.

"You are, darling," Cat drawled. "I never thought you had it in you, to be honest. Goodness, was it my good influence? I do believe that I feel proud."

"Me too," Danni said. "You haven't gotten any since time out of mind, but when you break out, I gotta say, you do it in style."

"Y'all need to quit," I said, getting embarrassed.

"Details, details," Cat said. "Is he as hot as he looks?"

A smile curved my lips. "Oh, yes."

"I think I'm jealous," Cat said.

"Girl, what's wrong with your neck?" Danni said, getting up and approaching me on the couch. She squatted down and sucked air through her teeth. "Damn, it looks like you let a pit bull gnaw on your neck like it was a bone."

"It's not that bad. He gets a little carried away in the neck area, that's all."

Danni was scrutinizing the area, tilting my head. "That's more than a little carried away. He's broken the skin in several places."

"You're lying."

"I'm not. Get a mirror and see for yourself. It's around the back, so you wouldn't be able to see from the front easily. He actually bit your neck? Shit, Luby, that's freaky."

Cat moved in and looked at the back of my neck, squinting. "I see only one little puncture."

Little puncture? I reached back and tried to feel it. Danni slapped my hand away. "Don't. You'll infect it. See the lacerated areas," she said to Cat. "Do you have any Betadine? I'll clean it up."

I headed to the bathroom. "I'm going to get a mirror," I said. There was no way Jake bit through the skin of my neck.

Allen was lying on my bed, engrossed in his television show. I retrieved a hand mirror from my dresser and headed for the full-length mirror on the back of the door. I turned around and examined the back of my neck with the hand mirror. I flinched inside at the extent of the bruising. I didn't bruise easily. I peered closer. Okay, there could be a puncture wound, but that was ludicrous. It was likely a bug bite. My bruised neck was probably feast central for Kansas City, Missouri, mosquitoes.

I moved to my medicine cabinet to get some hydrogen peroxide to clean my neck, but then hesitated. Instead I studied the pattern of bruises carefully.

Allen looked up at me as I came from the bathroom. I smiled at him briefly and went to my chest of drawers to get a bandanna. I tied it jauntily around my neck and returned to the living room. Cat and Danni were talking quietly.

I returned to my seat. Their gazes went straight to the bandanna at my neck.

"It could be a bug bite," I said. "I'm going over to his place for dinner. I'll talk to him then."

Both Cat and Danni still looked too worried.

"He's good to me, y'all. He's passionate in bed. It's cool. Really."

Cat stood. "I'd better get. With Darryl gone tonight, I planned to go to the gym and get in some primo DVD and novel reading down time."

"Did you talk to Darryl?" I asked.

She didn't meet my eyes. "Not yet, but I will." She regarded Danni. "Darryl always has good things to say about you. If I weren't so damned secure, or if I gave a damn, I'd be jealous. He's the sort of man you need to be hooking up with, instead of no-good dawgs like Marcus."

Danni said nothing, her facial expression shuttered.

"You heard from Marcus?" I asked. Here they were worrying about me when Cat's marriage was disintegrating and Danni was out of a car and in the middle of cutting loose the thug who caused her to lose it.

"Nope." Danni said. "My brother let me use one of his cars temporarily. What's killing me is that I'm going to have to pay all this money to get my car out of impound when they finally decide to release it—and the car payments don't stop."

"If you pressed charges against Marcus, insurance would help you out."

Danni gave a tight shake of her head. If she got back with Marcus . . . I thought of Allen and a rush of anger flew through me. "Danni, do you remember that you have a son in there? A black son who needs a decent role model? He doesn't need to be exposed to no-working, crime-dependent thugs."

"Amen to that," Cat added.

"I know." She looked out my window. "Marcus is history. It's that . . . I don't do well without a man around. And that's the sort of men who seem to like me."

"Bullshit," Cat said, surprising me. "All sorts of men hit on you, decent men. You offer yourself up on a silver platter to—"

"You know the deal," Danni said flatly to Cat, her normally light and pleasant voice gone dead and harsh.

I was astonished to see Cat pull back. "Yeah, I guess I do," she said. "But it's a damn shame."

"C'mon Allen, we're going," Danni called.

"You don't have to leave," I said.

"Yes, I do. And you be careful, girl. Don't let some good dick mess you up." Her face looked weary and defeated. "You don't want to be like me."

Cat reached out and hugged her. Danni leaned against her for a moment soaking up the affection and support. Then Allen came out of my room and a moment later they were gone.

I frowned. Cat may know the deal with Danni, but I sure didn't. My hand crept up to my neck. Be careful, she'd said. That was one thing I always tried to do.

My eyes widened in surprise as Jake let me into his apartment. What had been an empty space with only a sleeping bag on the floor had been transformed. Carpet that looked like the pelts of some black furred beast covered the floor. He had furnished the living room with a black leather couch and two matching oversized chairs and ottomans. One wall was covered with a large picture of a beautiful nude woman with black hair, her head thrown back in abandon. It looked old. I moved closer, and saw it was an oil painting on canvas that wasn't a reproduction. Then I drew in a sharp breath when I saw the dark substance she was lying in on the white-tiled floor . . . it was blood? In an instant a charming, baroque painting was transformed into something rather sinister.

"Do you like it?" Jake said, near my ear. He handed me a glass and I sipped it without looking at the contents. It was a martini, sophisticated, dry and perfect. Too much like him.

I nodded at his question.

"It's my grandmother, several greats removed, an original painted by my great-plus grandfather. Their story is very romantic," he said.

"Is that blood she's lying in?" The question slipped out.

"It could be, I suppose. But don't worry; she lived to a very old age." He sipped his own drink. "My family tends to be long-lived."

I tore my gaze away from the portrait on the wall and looked over at the opposite wall with its large screen plasma television and state-of-the-art stereo system he'd somehow purchased and installed in this short time.

"You've been busy," I said. The aroma from the kitchen made my stomach growl audibly. "And it smells delicious in here."

"Not as delicious as you look," he said. His green eyes caressed my body, along with the rough silk embrace of his voice. My mouth dried at his unmistakable meaning. "I want to show you something. Come with me."

He moved to the second bedroom, that he'd apparently transformed into an office. A large desk stood against the wall with a computer and a large flat screen monitor on it. Jake must have dropped thousands and thousands of dollars in a few days on all this.

There was something covered with a white sheet in the room. He drew me toward it and pulled away the sheet with a flourish. I gasped. There was an easel with a portrait of me on it. A me I barely recognized. My hair flowed over my shoulders like a woolen black cloud, my eyes were large and luminous, and my lips a cupid's bow made for kissing. Did I really look like that?

But it was my body that caught my breath in my throat. He portrayed me as a brown satin Venus, all curves and feminine hollows—a body made for loving.

"Do you like it? I'm not finished yet." There was a touch of anxiety in his voice that made him even more appealing if such a thing were possible.

I felt as if he'd punched me in the stomach—that was how overwhelmed I was at this tangible evidence of his regard for me. "Is that how you see me?" I asked in wonder.

He gathered me to him. "That's exactly how you are," he said and his lips finally caught mine.

I surrendered without a whimper, being only friends and personal ads forgotten. Our tongues mingled and his smoky cinnamon taste and scent washed over me. His kisses were tender, almost worshipful, and in no way friend-like.

"We'll fill our stomachs first. The night is young," he said as he raised his head, his voice hoarse.

I heard him with regret because I was juice-soaked and ready to receive him inside me. I'd never imagined a man's kiss could be as potent as making love with a lesser man. My empty stomach seemed unimportant in comparison to my sharp desire for Jake to fill the more intimate place.

But I pulled myself together and asked, "What did you cook?"

"I hope you like lamb," he said.

"I love it."

He served me a sumptuous meal of braised lamb chops with a clever sauce, sublime stuffed mushrooms, and tiny new potatoes. My heart flipped over. The man could cook like a god. Was this true love or what? The way to my heart wasn't only via my nether region.

"We have a tradition in my family. It's a little odd, but it would please me if you'd acquiesce." Jake sounded hesitant. Surely the man knew by now if he asked me to stand on my head and wave my legs in the air, I'd be bending over right now?

He uncorked a bottle of red wine. I know nothing about wine, but it looked expensive. "It's a special toast," he said. "Sealed by blood."

I didn't hear him right. "What?"

He poured two glasses of wine and picked up a knife. I focused on its sharp point. He didn't say what I thought I heard, did he?

"Sealed by blood," he said and raised the knife.

I have too much sista in me for my feet not to fail me on occasions such as this, so I was halfway to the door when I noticed that he'd pricked his finger with the knife.

I stopped my headlong flight.

"Relax," he said. "It's a strange custom, but not harmful."

He dropped a fat drop of blood into my glass of wine, then lifted it and held it out to me.

He had to be kidding. I moved slowly back to the table and took the glass from his hand. I peered into its depths. There was no trace of his blood, only swirling liquid depths of red wine. "We wear condoms to protect ourselves against disease transmitted by bodily fluids, and you want me to drink your blood?"

"The alcohol in the wine would kill any fragile microorganisms such as HIV."

I frowned, remembering that I'd read somewhere that the hepatitis virus wasn't all that fragile and alcohol didn't touch it.

"Please," he said. "I'm disease free, I promise. And it means a lot to me. Sort of as if you're my blood sister."

Being any sort of sister to him would be awfully incestuous, but I raised the glass to my lips. Under some potent spell he wound around me, I couldn't refuse him anything. The wine ran down my throat like red velvet. It hit my stomach and brain at the same time with an instant buzz.

He refilled my glass. I didn't look to see if he did the blood thingy. We picked up our utensils and ate. The food was good. It was as if I were high. The food was almost as good as sex. Every sense I had was heightened, and if it wasn't insane, I'd swear that a faint haze of red overlaid everything.

I'd cleaned my plate and the wine bottle was empty. I barely knew how it happened.

Jake pushed his plate aside and circled to my side of the table, holding out his hand to help me up. I got to my feet, feeling more satiated than I ever had before.

"You're mine," he said, tones of undeniable triumph ringing in his voice. I swayed into his arms. Did he have any doubt?

He waved his hands and music floated around us. I wondered how he did that trick and meant to ask him about it, but my mind seemed filled with cotton clouds. Nothing was definite; reality wavered as if edged in red.

Inner alarms were ringing, but I chose not to heed them as he moved my body to the richly textured classical sounds.

I wrapped my arms around his waist and dropped into a red mist of slow, passion-drugged bloodwine kisses. I lost myself.

We tugged away each other's clothes as we stumbled to the bedroom, evaporating the annoying obstacles between our skins.

Skin against skin, honey dipped in chocolate. Jake circled my nipple with his lips and sucked, gently pulling. I groaned as he pulled the heat up from my pussy. I pulled his head closer and arched my body, grinding my clit against his hard dick.

He moved his head to my other nipple and circled it with his tongue before he gave it another hard suck, while his hands worked my panties off. Ah, so good.

He lifted me and we fell on his bed, without missing a beat in the grind. I pulled him free from his briefs. His penis sprang out hard with a drop of pre-cum on the swollen tip. I circled it with my thumb, loving this part of him.

He growled and pushed me back on the bed, kneeling between my legs.

I drew in a sharp breath as Jake moved his head between my legs. I wanted to close them and draw away, embarrassed, but he didn't let me.

"You're lovely," he said. And his tongue worked magic. *Damn.* It was as good as my showerhead. No. Much, much better.

Thought fled from pure sensation as my fingers grasped and pulled at the sheets and my head tossed from side to side. My throat worked, emitting whimpers as the syrupy heat grew from my clit and filled my entire body. If he stopped what he was doing I would die.

Then I did die a small death. Everything went black and I stiffened as lava-hot molten pleasure rushed through in waves that I feared would tear me apart.

I'd barely caught my breath when Jake flipped me over with a savage sound and sank his dick deep in my pussy from behind. His hands grasped my breasts and his raspy thumbs massaged my nipples.

He sank his cock in slow, but rocking it hard and deep. God, it was good inside me.

I rocked and rolled against his plunging dick, tilting my hips to draw him in deeper. I rotated my hips around his hard cock, feeling the tip beat against my cervix, the ridge of its cut head making sweet friction up and down my pussy walls.

He reached and spread the juice from my dripping pussy to finger my swollen clit. Was that me making all that noise?

Fuck me, baby, oh god, don't stop, give it, give it . . . aww, so goddamn good.

He gave it. This was our special slow dance, no music needed. I heard him yell too as the convulsions seemed to start at my heart and work out toward my pussy, grasping and squeezing his cock in the throes of an orgasm that milked him dry.

Afterwards, as we lay together in comfortable silence, I turned on my side and looked at his profile. Such a beautiful man. Passionate danger mixed with a vulnerable sweet gentleness. He'd be deadly to any woman's heart.

There was a faint lingering hint of soreness in my neck. I touched the back of my neck with my fingers and stared at my hand in the dim light. It had come away marked with dark streaks. I lifted my hand to my mouth and tasted. Blood. My own.

PART TWO

"Reality slipped sideways, and my heart slid with it."
—Jake, Luby

CHAPTER 7

For I am sick of love.
—Song of Songs, 2:5

I am not crazy. I refuse to be crazy. Only a crazy bitch would let some motherfucker, no matter how goddamn fine, chew on her neck like she was a heap of steak tartare.

Only seriously crazy motherfuckers gnaw on other people's necks, I was fairly certain.

As for crazy motherfuckers, the sistas' handbook said that there was only one way to handle them. That one way was to get the fuck far away from them.

I rolled out of the bed and tried to find my panties, gave up, and pulled my jeans over my hips.

"What are you doing?" Jake asked.

"Finding my clothes. I remembered I, uh, left the iron on."

Sistas' handbook rule number two was that it is not wise to confront the crazy motherfucker without a door and a secure lock between you.

"You'll be back soon." He didn't ask, but said it as a certainty. Yeah, right.

"Yeah," I said, pulling my blue blouse over my head. I couldn't find my bra either. Oh, well. I patted my jeans pocket and felt the solid, sane reality of my house keys. "I'll be right back," I said. Then I fled.

I made it through my door, drew the deadbolt before the sobs started. There was no bigger fool in the world than me. I needed help. I remembered that Darryl was at the fire station tonight, so I picked up the phone and called Cat, barely able to see the numbers on the phone through my tears. My instinct was that I didn't want to be alone. Couldn't be alone. Or I'd go back to him. And if I stayed here, he'd come to me.

"Cat, can I come down to your place?"

"What's wrong?" she asked. "You sound terrible."

"Will you open the door for me? I'll be there in a minute."

"C'mon. I'll be waiting."

She was waiting at the door in a thick white terry cloth robe, looking worried. "What's the matter, Luby? You have me worried sick."

She pulled me in and closed and locked the door after me.

"Is somebody after you?" she asked.

Unsteeled against her concern, I threw myself on Cat's couch and dissolved into tears again.

"He bit my neck!" I wailed.

"Well, fuck me," Cat said, handing me a box of tissues.

I blew my nose. "No, he fucked me. But I drank his blood first, right before our delicious lamb dinner."

Cat's brows drew together. "You're making no sense. You drank his blood? What were y'all doing? Playing vampire?"

"He bit my neck!" I wailed again. "He's crazy, I know he's crazy."

"Sounds like you both are into some crazy shit," Cat said.

"Oh God, oh God, oh God."

"Calm down, girl. If it's that bad, you can get a restraining order. You're a lawyer. I know you can handle him."

I pounded my chest. "I might be able to handle him, but how can I handle me? I love him!"

I didn't look at Cat, because I know her well enough to know she was barely restraining herself from rolling her eyes.

"I'm going to call him and tell him it's over now, while I can," I said, panting.

Cat handed me the phone.

I punched in his number on my cell with trembling fingers.

"I missed you," he said.

"How could you?" I asked.

"What?"

"You bit me on the neck!" I wailed.

Silence. Silence. Silence.

"What do you have to say?" I finally asked.

"Tastes good, less filling?" he said.

"That's it. I'm hanging up and I never want to see your insane, neck-biting—"

"Hold on. We need to talk."

"Talk? Newsflash: Biting negates conversation. You bit me on the neck!"

"I think you've established that to yourself now, no need to keep saying it. Come over and we'll sit down—"

"And let you bite me on the neck again? You bit me on the neck!"

Cat took the phone from me. "Sit down, Luby. You're on a repeating loop." She lifted it to her ear. "Did you bite Luby or not and why?" she asked. He said something.

"Yeah," she said. "But that's not answering my question."

I studied my feet. Nice, small feet, real far away from my neck.

"Okay, yeah. Yeah, it's some freaky shit," Cat said.

Feet were important, but they didn't have nearly as many important structures running through them as a neck.

"She's real upset and I can't blame her. Yeah. I guess I could do that. Okay." Then she hung up. "Don't go anywhere," Cat told me sternly and swept into her bedroom.

I could deal with a foot fetish freak. A little toe nibbling never hurt anyone. But my neck! I mused about my feet until Cat came out of her bedroom dressed in jeans and a T-shirt.

"Poor baby, you're shell-shocked." Cat held out her hand to me and pulled me up from my prone position on her couch. "Let's go."

I knew she was taking me to Jake's. He'd talked her into it. I wasn't surprised. He was charming. He was sexy. I drank his blood with nary a qualm. Well, maybe only a couple of qualms. I didn't bother to protest and I was going to die from hepatitis Z after blood drinking and neck chewing.

But despite everything, I wanted to see him, wanted him to prove to me that he wasn't crazy and the biting holes in my neck was only a big joke.

"Hold up," Cat said. She reached behind the television on the entertainment center and pulled out a pistol. I was astonished. I thought that Cat had more sense than to keep firearms in the home the way she and Darryl fought all the time. Did she want to spend the rest of her productive adult years in prison for killing the man? What was wrong with her?

I followed Cat meekly to Jake's door. She raised her fist to pound on it, but he opened it before the blow landed.

"Come," he said. "I have something to confess."

Oh shit, confession didn't sound like it went with convincing me that he's not really a crazy motherfucker.

I felt Cat give a little shudder as she brushed past him to enter his apartment, pulling me close behind her.

I straightened, and led the way to the couch, well aware of Jake's sexual pull. He'd opened another bottle of wine and followed us with a glass in hand. "Can I get you ladies something to drink?"

"No." Cat said shortly. "You said you had something to say that would explain the marks on Luby's neck."

He shrugged and sat in one of the leather chairs adjacent to us, took a sip of wine. On the surface he looked relaxed, but I sensed a deep unease emanating from him.

"Are you sexually attracted to me at this moment?" he asked Cat.

Girlfriend actually sputtered. "That's hardly an appropriate question."

"I agree. Nevertheless, are you?"

"I'm not here to answer wack-ass questions," Cat said. I noticed that she wasn't meeting his eyes and didn't look in my direction once. I'd bet money she was nearly ready to rape him. I felt no jealousy, only a wry amusement. I knew exactly what she was feeling.

"Don't you think it's a little odd?" Jake asked. "Here you are, indignant over my treatment of your friend, but as soon as you enter my house all you can think of is having sex with me. My body covering yours, my lips tasting your skin."

Okay, he was going too far now.

Cat licked her lips. "Maybe we better go," she said to me. "He doesn't have anything worthwhile to say."

"But I do," he said. "The explanation for how you feel is simple. I'm not like you, not wholly human."

I sighed, and nodded in assent at Cat. "Yeah, let's go." He was making it worse, ripping open the hole in my heart with his teeth.

81

"I hate using the word vampire," he continued. "Because it's not accurate at all, but—"

Tears were stinging my eyes. The love of my life was nuttier than my fruitcake mother. Talk about my bad fucking luck.

Cat drew me to my feet.

"You can leave," he told her. "I appreciate you bringing her here. And by the way, you'll remember nothing from the moment before Luby contacted you. You'll awake refreshed in your bed tomorrow."

Then to my astonishment, Cat nodded and walked toward the front door.

"Cat! What are you doing?" I said, utterly shocked.

"I'm going home," she said. There was a vacant look in her eyes that scared me. She walked around me and out the door, closing it softly behind her.

I swung around to Jake. "What did you do to her?" I demanded.

He ran an exasperated hand through his hair. "Nothing but what I said. She'll forget and wake up tomorrow as if nothing has happened." He frowned down at me. "I knew you wouldn't come unless she brought you. Can we talk now?" he said, his voice slightly peeved.

I crossed my arms and poised my neck ready to swivel, allowing my anger to mask my fear. "Talk," I said.

"I'm really sorry I bit you. I lost control, the pleasure we shared was too intense. Are you in pain?"

I shook my head. I could buy a passionate lover's abandoned and thoughtless love nips, but what about the crazy? "You're a wannabe vampire, right?" I said, my tone dripping sarcasm.

"I was wrong to take you without explaining the situation to you," he said. "Luby, the second I saw you, I recognized you for what you are."

"And what is that?"

"You are my mate—and one of us."

I edged toward the door.

"Stop it," he said. "We're bonded. You knew something special was going on. Something far different than you ever experienced before, yet it felt exactly right."

"You do realize that I have a crazy mother? Are you aware of my low tolerance for insanity? You're not taking me there, you crazy motherfucker." I darted to the door and pulled it open. "Come near me again and I'll file for a restraining order." I shut the door behind me with a satisfying slam and took off at a dead run.

Somehow, I knew that he wouldn't follow. My relief was mixed with deep sadness and an unsettled empty feeling.

I only hoped I'd soon be able to chalk up my brief time with Jake as a learning experience. I doubted it, though. He'd affected me more than I wanted to acknowledge. What really hurt was that I knew it was more than the dick—I'd actually cared for him.

I went straight to Cat's and knocked on the door. I was going to read her the riot act for abandoning me to a man who could well have been a nutcase serial killer. I knew with almost every cell of my body that Jake wouldn't hurt me, but Cat couldn't know that.

I knocked on her door and she didn't answer. I banged harder. "Hold your goddamn horse," she called in a sleepy voice.

Cat pulled open the door, covering a huge yawn with her hand. "It's after midnight. What's up with you banging on my door without calling to wake me up first?" she asked.

My jaw dropped.

"Cat, I was over here a few minutes ago. You took me to Jake's apartment!"

She squinted at me. "What have you been smoking? I haven't seen you since earlier this evening before you went over to Jake's place for dinner. What's up, Luby?"

I backed away, stunned amazement zooming through me. "Uh, nothing. I'll see you tomorrow, okay?"

"Jesus. I'm going back to bed. And call me before you come banging on my door after midnight for no reason." With those words she closed her door.

I stared at it for a few minutes, my heart pounding. Somehow Jake had made her forget everything. How did he do that? It made no sense. Then came the worst thought—what if I were the crazy one after all?

CHAPTER 8

As the apple tree among the trees of the woods . . .
—Song of Songs, 2:3

I woke up that Saturday morning with a deep ache inside. I couldn't remember for a moment where it came from. Then the events of last night came flooding back. I closed my eyes against the rush of emotion that accompanied my memories.

A treacherous voice whispered, *if you and Jake are both as crazy as June bugs, why can't you be crazy together?*

I reached for the phone and called Cat. "What's up?" she chirped, all goddamn cheery and bright.

"Do you remember what happened last night with Jake?" I asked.

"I remember you banging on my door after midnight. Sorry I was grumpy, but you know I'm no good when my beauty sleep is interrupted. What's going on with you and Jake?"

She didn't remember. My stomach dropped like an elevator. "We broke up," I said.

"Oh no! You two were good together. Serious, Luby, I haven't seen you as happy and glowing in ages. Are you sure you can't salvage it?"

Nope, she didn't remember a thing about me being neck chewed and Jake telling us he was a vampire. So that meant that Cat was crazy too.

Or what Jake said was true.

"I'm pretty sure it's over. Oops, there's my grandma on the other line," I lied. "I'll get back to you later."

I hung up, and rolled out of bed. Somehow it was easier to deal with everybody being crazy than that crazy shit around me being true.

The phone rang, I eyed the caller ID. It was Jake. I let the answering machine get it.

"I know you're home," he said. "I just wanted to let you know, that when you're ready, I'm here. I'm not going anywhere."

I waited expectantly, but there was the soft click of his phone being put back in its cradle and that was all.

I swallowed hard. If I overlooked the neck chewing and the request that I drink his blood, he was the most outwardly stable man I'd met in recent memory.

But you have to admit that neck chewing and blood drinking negates a shitload of sanity.

Grandma was waiting for me. I sighed and headed for the shower. My problems weren't going anywhere, and I'd best get ready and face my day.

Grandma was lying on the couch when I went into the house, such an unusual position for her, I was immediately alarmed.

She got up as soon as she heard me come through the door and looked at me apologetically. "I'm not getting any younger, child."

"Just as long as you don't get older, we're cool," I said, not really joking. I couldn't bear it if something happened to Grandma.

"Have you had breakfast yet?" she asked.

"No, I haven't eaten, but I'm not very hungry."

She gave me a keen look. "Come and have a cup of coffee with me and tell me what's going on with you."

A few minutes later, settled at the table with Grandma, who'd managed to persuade me to have a piece of her fabulous peach cobbler and a cup of coffee with lots of half-and-half, I was at a loss at where to start.

But Grandma solved my dilemma and started for me. "You haven't mentioned what we talked about last week," she said.

"What's that?" I said, savoring a piece of peach cobbler. What did Grandma put in this stuff? Ambrosia of gods? I'd weigh over two hundred pounds if I still lived here, too many years past my childhood's fast metabolism.

"When I told you what's going to happen after you turn twenty-seven."

The fork paused in my mouth and all of a sudden the cobbler felt leaden in my stomach.

"Grandma, you didn't tell me anything that made much sense."

"Such things rarely make sense. They simply are." She lifted her cup, her sharp eyes assessing me over the rim. "It's a man, isn't it?" she asked. "Like your mother said."

Like my mother said? Then the memory returned. *You wanted to fuck him, didn't you, little bitch? And you will. Be careful, little bitch, because it'll be the death of you.*

My God. She was telling me about Jake. I touched my bruised neck under the bandanna I'd tied around it.

"Awfully warm to be wearing a scarf," Grandma said.

"It is a man," I said, my words emerging from my throat slowly and painfully. "I need to know whether what Lily said about him is true." I unwrapped the bandanna and laid it on the table.

Grandma's eyes narrowed infinitesimally. "I don't think I've ever told you about your daddy," she said.

Why did she think I needed or wanted to hear about my daddy? I'd asked her about Jake.

She got up from the table. "Do you want some more cobbler?" she asked.

She took her time, serving herself a generous piece of cobbler and freshening our coffee before she sat down.

"He was a handsome man, delicate featured and compact, with large eyes and a mobile mouth, not too tall. He looked a lot like you, child."

"I've heard," I said, hiding my sour expression in my coffee.

"You haven't heard everything. He was from New Orleans, an old family. He was a priest."

This was new. "He was a Catholic priest?"

"No child. A Santería priest."

I searched my brain for what scant information I had on Santería. "Great. Another insane relative who sacrifices chickens to the gods like the gods can't go to Kentucky Fried like everybody else does."

"You've been hurt badly by your mother. Don't take it out on your world." She pulled out a folded piece of paper from her pocket. "Your father wanted you to have this when you were twenty-seven, but I think you need it now."

I smoothed out the aged and crumpled piece of paper. The following words were highlighted:

The sacred world of Santería is motivated by ashe. Ashe is growth, the force toward completeness and divinity. The real world is one of pure movement. In fact, the real world is one not of objects at all but of forces in continual process.

"Mumbo jumbo."

"It's not mumbo jumbo. It is about the principle underlying the use of magic. All magic."

I didn't realize that I'd spoken aloud. I sat back in my chair and stared at Grandma. "Jake believes in magic," I said. "He said he's not human, but a vampire. He bit my neck." I pointed. "You're telling me that he's not crazy, that I am?" Near the end of my speech, my voice started to waver. I felt utterly ashamed when I realized that I couldn't stop the tears dripping from my eyes.

"I'm trying to tell you that you're not crazy. I'm telling you about the world beyond this world. The one you fear so much." She leaned forward, her rheumy eyes blazing with an inner light. "I'm trying to tell you that it's real and you need to deal with it."

The tears only dripped faster.

Grandma sighed. "I wanted to give you a spiritual foundation, a real faith. I feel as if I failed."

"What does my faith in God have to do with this . . . " I'd never curse in front of Grandma, no matter how upset. "Stuff," I finished. "You tell me about ghosts and divination, about vampires and a voodoo priest for a father whose sole paternal legacy is a page torn from a book with mumbo jumbo highlighted. What the heck does that have to do with faith?"

"Ashe is the energy of the universe, the substance of magic, all magic, from the heart light of the Christ to the Santería rites. Learn what ashe is, manipulate it and hold it, and you can control your destiny."

I didn't raise my eyes from my creamy coffee. Dread crawled through me like a living thing. Grandma's voice filled the room with ringing tones. Truth, which reverberated through her voice. She believed in magic and she sounded insane. Passionate insane.

"Fear is the ultimate evil and you are filled with it. Face your fears and release them."

I moaned and buried my face in my hands.

But Grandma wouldn't stop, her words lashing at me as if they were whips. "I've sheltered you too much. Made you afraid of any reality that threatens your small world. Look at me, Luby Uniquoncie. Look at me!" she thundered.

I raised my head and gasped when I saw Grandma surrounded by a halo of shifting colors—pink, gold, green, and white. My heart felt as if it was going to explode in my chest. Everything dimmed as my head expanded and I felt myself slipping—

"Don't you dare faint!" Grandmother ordered me sharply. "I know I didn't raise that much of a coward."

My head snapped up. "What is it?" I asked.

"Something all things share, my energy matrix. Some call it an aura. This is the smallest slice of what your father was trying to let you know, everything is energy—and we have the gift to be able to manipulate energy in greater or lesser ways."

"Please, please turn it off," I almost pleaded.

"Why, are you afraid?"

"No, I'm not afraid." I tried to swallow the giant lump in my throat that was evidence otherwise. "I'm overwhelmed."

I tried to sort through what my grandmother was trying to tell me, verbal and nonverbal as her aura gradually faded.

The birds chirped, the sun shone through the windows and it looked as normal a summer Saturday morning as it had fifteen minutes ago. But everything had changed as much as if a cataclysm caused all I knew to lay in ruins.

"You're telling me that vampires, witches, and ghosts exist? That magic is. And that my mother isn't really crazy?"

"Your mother is crazy enough. You have enough of her traits to frighten me. She never could face the reality of things enough to deal with them. Soon she could deal with nothing, not even her own life."

Grandma couldn't have said anything that would've hurt me more—that I was like my mother. I know the pain was raw on my face, but she took a breath and continued on.

"Your mother hears the spirits. She told me some things that I think are truths. First, I want to let you know that I believe your young man is the same as you are."

"He said I was like him." Did that mean I was a vampire and doomed to run around in ugly black leather, shrinking from crosses and drinking blood? I didn't see how. I don't even like liquid meal replacement drinks. "He's a vampire." I tried to be straightforward and blasé when I said it to my grandma, but you understand it was hard as fuck to utter the words as fact.

"No vampire can make true love with a human," Grandma said. "They're demons, beings who reside mainly in the astral sphere. Creatures such as that can no longer clothe themselves permanently in flesh."

I barely could wrap my mind around the fact that Grandma didn't deny the existence of vampires and mentioned demons in the same breath. I had no clue about *the astral sphere* or the other stuff. But I decided to be proactive. Obviously she was informed on such matters, matters that I once referred to only as *freaky shit.* "He bit me on the neck. I think he drank my blood. And he wanted me to taste his, a drop."

She drew in a breath. "You didn't tell me that."

"Grandma, I just told you of his existence."

She waved me silent, preoccupied in thought. "He bonded you to him." She looked worried.

"And what's this that Lily said about him being the death of me?"

"I didn't see this man ever hurting you, but I did see that knowing him could put you under some sort of threat."

"Death is a pretty major threat. And his tendency to gnaw on my neck is rather unfortunate."

Grandma looked at me in surprise, then threw back her head and laughed.

CHAPTER 9

"I'm happy that I entertain you," I said to Grandma, and I admit that I said it somewhat sulkily.

"I'm sorry, baby," she said, wiping her eyes. "It was funny."

"I don't think being bitten on the neck is in the least funny. And if I'm like him as he says, I'm not looking forward to the monotonous liquid diet."

My eyes narrowed when Grandma looked as if she wanted to laugh again.

"He's human, child. He's not going to drain you dry. Nor does he live only on blood or would be burned to a crisp by the sun. Those are fairy tales."

"Weren't you just asking me to accept all manner of fairy tales?"

"No. I was asking you to have faith. Faith is the substance of things hoped for, the evidence of things not seen. Substance and evidence are tangible and reality-based. There is no need to take flights of fancy, or fear insanity. What I want you to accept are merely unacknowledged parts of the natural world."

She got the coffeepot and refilled her cup again, offering me some. I shook my head and she reached for the cream and sugar. "Most of today's legends and myths are based in the realities of an ancient world. Few peoples of that world survived, but remnants of their blood remain in humans down to this day.

"There are great families, witch families some call them, who practice magical arts. Some hold great power in the world, manipulating governments, world finance and multinational corporations.

"Some keep a low profile. But they're all interested in not diluting their magical bloodlines. Most choose to mate only with others of a similar kind and some have no choice, but must do so if they want their seed to be fruitful."

"So you're saying the world is run by witches?"

"A totally inaccurate word. I would prefer to call them, um, people of power. That has a good sound, don't you think?"

She stirred the liquid in her cup until it was pale beige. "They don't run the world, I'd say they probably manage a generous portion. The most powerful ones keep to themselves though. Some are unknowing of their heritage and many reside in far-flung great families. Your Jake is certainly one of these people."

"And I'm one too?"

Grandma lifted the cup to her lips. "I believe we are." I blinked at her in disbelief.

"My daughter told me that there was once a race of people, snake or dragon people many called them," she continued. "They drank the blood of living things to sustain them. A human with this trait has an affinity toward blood, among other possible talents. In your young man's passion, he might have lost control."

"Why were you concerned that he wanted me to drink his blood when I first told you?"

"Why, I once saw the snake people in a dream performing a

similar bonding ritual, except that they exchanged great quantities of their blood. I believe that he's taken you as his life mate, child. Seems as if it would have been polite to tell you so first." She sucked her teeth. "It was like your father to pull something like that, to fixate on his mate and take her regardless."

"My father took my mother as his life mate? I thought he disapproved."

"He did, but she ran away from him while she was heavy with child, you. I don't think he would have let her leave him that easily though. He would have found her and come to get her. I was right. Years after she left him, she told me that she killed him."

I was taken aback, and then angry, then shattered. Why had no one told me? "It's true then, that she hates me because I remind her of him?"

Grandma shook her head. "Maybe, in part. But your mother's difficulty is she's always believed that you were going to kill *her*."

"What?"

"I told her that the spirits have it wrong, that such a thing is not possible and I've never had any visions of any such thing, but she won't believe me. You see, ever since you were born the spirits whisper death in her ears. They tell her that you're the tool of your father's revenge beyond the grave."

By then you can imagine the headache I had. Absorbing that my mother killed my father and hated me all my life because she thought I'd kill her, was a little much. "Are you about ready to go shopping?" I asked, desperate to change the subject.

"In a while. Why don't you go and take a couple of painkillers and lie on your bed for a while? Think things over. I'll call you when I'm ready."

She woke me from a light nap in an hour. We went shopping with no more talk of magic, visions, magical beings or mama killing. And although the direction of my life had again changed completely, the sun still shone, the birds still chirped, and it seemed like an entirely normal day.

It was early evening when I returned from Grandma's and I had to rush to dress. Danni and I were having our first online personally arranged blind date. We agreed to double up for the experiment. We were going to meet two men at a restaurant. I rushed to her apartment as we had arranged.

Cat opened the door. "She's almost ready, finishing her make-up. You look good. I'll only be a few minutes. C'mon and keep me company, okay?"

I sat on the bed with Cat while Danni stood in front of her dresser. "We need a signal," Danni said.

"A signal?" I echoed.

"We need to let each other know if we need rescuing." She bent close to the mirror to apply her mascara. "If things aren't going well, I'll put a finger on the right side of my nose. If the man is so bad I think I'm going to puke, I'll put my finger on the left side of my nose?"

"I personally think fingers and noses are indelicate. The guys are going to be watching to see if you start flicking boogers," Cat said.

"Ewwwww," I said. "I have to agree with Cat, fingers and nose signals aren't going to work."

"Cat isn't going with us. Did I ask you for your two cents, girl?" Danni asked.

"Nope, but I gave it, and see, Luby agrees."

"So what are we going to use as a signal if we want to get away from those guys?"

"How about a word?" I suggested.

"It would have to be a word common enough not to draw undue attention to itself," Danni said.

"But uncommon enough so you won't miss it in the flow of conversation," Cat added.

I thought for awhile, then my gaze fell on the flowers on Danni's bedside table. "How about vase?"

"Vase?"

"Yes. The restaurant will probably have vases on the tables, so we can work it into casual conversation. Nice vase, we can say."

"That's pretty good," Danni agreed. "Who talks about vases out on a date?" She laid the wand down with a flourish and surveyed her image in the mirror. "I'm ready."

"You two look wonderful," Cat said. "I want to know all the dirty details as soon as you get back. Hell, maybe next time I'll be going with you."

We'd got to the restaurant right on time and were seated. We figured the guys probably came early to check us out and bolt if we were hideous.

We were right. We'd started on our first glass of wine when two black guys approached our table from the bar. They were dressed appropriately in slacks and sports jackets, casual, but not too casual.

They both knew not to show up with raggedy, unpolished, fake leather shoes. They wore decent shoes with spit shines. I checked out their shoes before I looked into their faces closely. The face can lie, but most men don't realize how much the choice and care of his footwear say about his character. They could be as fine as hell, but if they had scuffed shoes it wouldn't matter.

Acceptable, I thought, until I saw the roses they both carried. Not real roses mind you, but fake roses, the ones made out of polyester and plastic.

"You must be Danielle," one said to Danni. "You have the most astounding eyes."

He sat across from her and the other guy took the chair across from me. Danni and I tried not to look at each other and roll our eyes as they handed us each a fake rose with a flourish.

"I'm Bill. The engineer," he added and waited espectantly for my response.

"Uh, thanks for the rose. I'm Luby Jones." I extended my hand.

"This is Michael. He's a lawyer too," Bill said. "He turned to Danni. "And you must be Danielle. You're a registered nurse, correct?"

I wanted to roll my eyes. Work titles were damn important to these guys.

Danni didn't look impressed either. I wasn't surprised because the professional types I insisted on choosing weren't her cup of tea. "I'm an LPN," she said.

The guy across from her, Michael, had the nerve to look crestfallen. "When you said you were a nurse, I assumed you meant a real nurse," he said.

CHAPTER 10

Until the day breaks, and the shadows flee away . . .
—Song of Songs, 2:17

Nope, I'm not joking. He told hardworking, feet-hurting, bedpan schlepping Danni that she wasn't a real nurse. I saw her jaw tighten, but she didn't say a word.

Then Michael decided to assess the size of my breasts, which even with Danni's implants were larger than hers. I could see the equation working in his mind, boobs or not, boobs or not.

Then he turned his attention from my boobs and grinned in Danni's face. I guess she won, poor thing.

They both were decent-looking. Bill was red bone, with nice teeth, good bone structure, average build, and height. In his correspondence, he assured me he was a Christian. I glanced over at the other one. He was about the same, but darker and a bit taller.

We studied our menus. Engrossed in choosing either penne pasta primavera or a Caesar salad, I was slow to notice that Bill was talking to me. "It's important to have pride in your image," he said.

"I guess," I said. What did that have to do with anything I wondered.

"I think both husband and wife being working professionals are essential to affording the image that matters. Don't you agree?" He looked at me in anticipation.

The image that matters? What was he talking about? Did I miss something? I must have missed a lot. I looked toward Danni. She gave a tiny shrug.

"I agree," Michael said. "It is so hard for a couple to lay a solid economic foundation nowadays. It takes effort, hard work, and most of all, investment."

"Investment?" Danni echoed, now looking as perplexed as I felt.

"Oh yes. I'm a member of the Black Republican Investment Association."

Oh Lawd, he was like a chocolate-flavored version of her father and brother. He might as well have stood up and gone home right then as far as Danni was concerned.

"Hmmmm," she said. "Interesting." She had that *tone* in her voice. "I think couples should work hard toward self-sufficiency too," she said.

They both perked up. What was wrong with these fools?

"Since I don't have a real profession, my dream is to live in a homestead in rural America or Canada with no electricity or running water, grow our own food and birth and home-school at least six more children, like my pioneer forbearers," Danni said.

I doubt if Bill and Michael could have looked more aghast if they tried. I tried not to crack up. Danni wouldn't even go camping if a hotel with room-service wasn't involved.

"So you see, I need to get a big buck that can chop lots of wood, pick our crops and to start the child birthing right away," Danni said, batting her eyelashes at Michael.

If Mr. Black Republican could have turned white, I think he would have. As it was he turned a nice shade of gray. Fortunately, the waiter arrived.

"Are you ready to order?" the waiter asked.

"Side salad with ranch on the side," Danni said without looking at the menu. I agreed with the message. We weren't staying long.

I opened my mouth to order the same thing when Bill asked, "What would you like to eat?"

"I was going to tell the waiter that I want a side salad with oil and vinegar also."

"Manners, manners," he chided.

Manners? What the fuck?

"She would like a side salad with a vinaigrette dressing," he told the waiter. "Would you like anything else?"

"Uh, no."

"And you, sir?" the waiter asked.

"Nothing. We're only having drinks. Bring a carafe of your house red."

Apparently they'd already made use of their signals and we didn't pass muster.

"It's difficult to find the right one, don't you agree?" Michael said.

"We wouldn't know yet, this is the first time we've done this," I said.

Bill chuckled. "You all say that."

"So many of them lie," Michael said. "Tell them what happened last weekend, Bill."

"These two women sent these attractive pictures of themselves, but when they showed up, they were whales." He shuddered.

"They lied," Michael added indignantly. "The first thing we asked them is why the pictures didn't match."

"And do you know what one of them said?" Bill asked.

Danni and I didn't answer, but he went on, as if we weren't there. "One of them said they wanted to allow us to get to know them before we made a judgment about them."

Mike snickered. "Who would want to get to know those blobs of blubber?"

"I was terrified somebody from work would see me with those pigs," Bill said.

Michael nodded in agreement.

Bill ran his eyes over our bodies. "You girls are nice and trim. I don't know why fatties bother. You can't do anything with them anyway until you roll 'em in flour and look for the wet spot."

Mike erupted in gales of laughter.

Danni looked horrified, but I couldn't take it another second. I started coughing until I was bent over double and Bill and Mike were looking around in embarrassment.

"Are you all right?" Danni asked.

"Vase, vase!" I croaked.

"That means she needs some water on her face," Danni told the men. "I need to help her to the bathroom."

We gathered our purses and made our way to the alcove where the restrooms were. We peered around the corner to the losers at our table.

"Ready to bounce?" I asked.

"Do you need to ask?" Danni replied. "They're not looking. Let's go, fast!"

We sprinted toward the front door.

"I've become ill. The gentlemen at our table will take care of the check," I said to the maître d' as we hurried past him. He looked bored and waved us on.

We cleared the front door and ran like hell to my car.

"Drive, drive!" Danni shrieked.

I burned rubber out of the parking lot.

A few blocks away, I slowed down. "I wanted to put those two guys in a roomful of fat women and let them whup their sorry asses until they screamed like little girls," I said.

"Word," Danni said with a grin. "Those were some trifling sumbitches. You're going to have to do this blind date shit on your own from now on. I'm not having it."

"I feel betrayed by the online dating service."

"Those assholes mainly wanted to cop some ass," Danni said. "A lot of dummies would be fooled by all that money bullshit they were spouting to impress. Thank God we didn't give them our last names or phone numbers."

I nodded. I didn't say it to Danni then, mainly because I didn't want to hear her and Cat say I told you so, since they both thought I was crazy to go out on Jake, but I knew my blind dating days were over too.

We'd barely made it back to my apartment before Cat came banging on my door.

"How was it?" she asked. "You two in love?"

"Please," Danni said. "We didn't even get as far as dinner." She went into the kitchen and I heard her rummaging around.

"It was a disaster," I told Cat. "We ended up literally bolting before dinner and barely escaped. Get this, one of the fools bragged to Danni that he was a member of the Black Republican Investment Association. She almost had a stroke."

Cat chuckled. "Told you so," she said.

"Bitch. Danni said she wasn't doing it anymore. Maybe you can talk her into including white guys in her search. There are millions of them and she'd have her pick."

"Danni's not going out with any white guy," Cat said.

"I'm sure not," Danni said, her arms loaded with Coke, beer, and everything that marginally resembled junk food in my kitchen.

"What is your deal, Danni? Cat seems to know and I don't."

She shrugged.

"Danni paid the babysitter for hours more. Maybe we could go out," Cat said. I knew she was changing the topic and helping Danni out of the need to answer. She shouldn't bother. If Danni didn't want to confide in me, I knew when to back off.

"Remember when you told me you saw my father at your job?" Danni asked.

I nodded.

"I hate his guts. I wish he was dead." The low ferocity of her voice took me aback. What could I say? Cat was looking off into the distance.

"You two don't know how lucky you were to grow up without a father," she continued. She swallowed. "He molested me, Luby, and so did my brother. I can't stand to have anything like their hands on me. I can't help it. It makes me feel like I want to throw up."

I wanted to say a lot of things to her. That there was help for her, that her father and brother deserved to die, that she shouldn't make a train wreck out of her life because she was a victim, but I said nothing. Her pain had to run deeper than I can fathom. Despite all the words that were available, there were only a very few that were appropriate. I searched for them a moment, found them. "I'm sorry, Danni," was what I said.

She nodded. "Thanks," she said.

We sat in silence and reached for the junk food Danni had piled on the coffee table. Inwardly, I was reeling at all the revelations I'd recently endured.

Danni's tragedy, what my grandma told me, what happened

with Jake yesterday. My mind crawled to standby, functioning mainly to get me through the day.

Danni yawned and stood. "I'm going home to enjoy some rare me time. I'll see you later, all right?"

"You knew about this all along?" I asked Cat as soon as Danni left.

"Yeah. She made me promise not to tell anybody. She had a really hard time, but she thinks she has her past under control."

"I guess she deals with what happened pretty well, considering. But I'm wondering why she's so attracted to the thugs?" I asked.

"I think when you go through something like that, although it's totally the adult's fault, a kid can't help blaming themselves on some level. How it affected her self-esteem is a side effect that Danni's less clear about. She probably would have been with sorry-ass white guys too, if she could tolerate white men."

"Geez," I said. "I want to hand her some names of excellent therapists but I don't dare. What kills me is that her father got away clean. And she said her brother molested her too. Damn. She still sees him occasionally."

"She told me she holds it together for her mother's sake."

"Her mother that didn't bother to protect her?"

"I had an idea for something that would be a win-win situation for both Danni and I. I'd like to run it past you," Cat said.

"As long as it doesn't take any mental energy that I don't have right now, sure," I said, stretching out on the couch.

"I want to give Darryl to Danni," Cat said.

I raised my head and stared at her.

CHAPTER 11

Many waters cannot quench love, nor can floods drown it.
—Song of Songs, 8:7

"Danni's wanted my husband for a long time," Cat said.
My head fell back against the couch. You know when you've had one of those days when it felt as if small and mischievous gods were fucking with you for a laugh?

Well, my day was shaping up to be worse than that. I raised my hand to glance at my watch and see how long I had until it was over.

"I've thought about it a long time. Darryl and Danni are a perfect match, and she deserves a shot at a good man."

I covered my eyes with my forearm. "I thought you couldn't stand Darryl and said you couldn't wait to divorce his sorry ass."

"I can't stand him, but that doesn't mean that he's not basically a good man. It's not like I'd marry a loser. We're sick of each other and were never well matched. I think it's a good thing that I realized this before we had children or heaven forbid, got old. But Darryl's still in denial."

"Denial?"

"Yeah. I went through the fire and dealt with my feelings of failure. I realize that the marriage is over and it isn't really any-one's fault, it's just the way it is. Darryl still has this tremendous feeling of frustration and anger. He's unhappy as hell but blames himself and blames me the most."

"What does this have to do with giving your husband to Danni? How do you know he wants her?"

"I've seen how he looks at her sometimes. He thinks she's hot as hell, and I know them both well. They'd be well-matched personality-wise for the long haul and they'd actually like each other. He's good with kids too and crazy about Allen. She's more practical than me and good with money. See, a win-win sit-uation."

"For them maybe, but what about you?"

"I get out of there clean and get to start over and reinvent my-self without the baggage. Plus think of all the good karma I'll generate."

I groaned and covered my face with a throw pillow. Cat ig-nored me.

"I've tried all week to bring up separation to Darryl and I can't get the words out. He's going to put all the shit for our marriage not working back on me when he's driving me insane too. So guess what?" she said.

"What?" I answered, my voice muffled by the pillow.

"I have this kick-ass plan to get them together." I moved the pillow to look at her. Cat rubbed her hands together in glee.

"You've given this a lot of thought? Christ, Cat."

"A humongous amount of thought. I wanted to run it past you, then I'll talk to Danni about it."

"What makes you think she'd agree to this . . . ?" I wanted to say crap, but figured that it would piss Cat off.

"I told you she has the hots for Darryl and has for years. If we weren't friends, she would have made a move on him ages ago, whether he was married or not. Now, listen."

Oh God. I covered my face up with the pillow again while I listened to Cat chatter happily to me about her crazy-ass plan.

After Cat left to go and convince Danni to take her husband off her hands, the phone rang. I raised my pounding head and looked at the caller ID. It was Jake. I ached to pick up the phone and tell him about everything my grandmother had said. I wanted to accept everything and fall into his arms and beg him to make love to me, neck chewing included or not. I wanted to drink his blood and give him mine.

But I did none of those things and the answering machine clicked on. He didn't leave a message. I dropped my clothes on the floor and climbed into bed without brushing my teeth or removing my makeup, three things I never do. Despite of all I wanted, right now I needed to sleep and collect my dazed emotions and garner my courage.

I pulled the covers over my head to keep all the demons, magic, ghosts, voodoo, and vampires out.

I slept so late on Sunday morning that I didn't have time to get ready for church. Usually Grandma would have called, but I guess she knew that I'd be wrung out from yesterday. She'd probably had one of her friends from church pick her up.

I stretched and got out of bed feeling refreshed and much better. Today I would talk to Jake, find out from him what was going on and go from there. There were a lot of things that I wanted to do. I wanted to see my father's family and confront my mother. I wanted to find out more of this world outside the world that Grandma told me about. The best thing was that I didn't feel crazy. I felt slightly apprehensive and excited, but not crazy. For the first time, I had a certainty that I wasn't my mother's daughter.

After I got dressed, I went in the kitchen and put on coffee and got a box of cereal off the shelf. Before I finished my first cup of coffee, there was a tap on the door, and I heard Cat's voice. "You there?"

I pulled open the door to her happy excited face. "Danni and I decided to do the confrontation thing with Darryl today. I'd like you to be there for moral support."

"The confrontation thing?"

"My sister agreed to say that she was sick. I told him that I had to leave for St. Louis immediately, and Danni would bring over dinner," she grinned. "I slept over at Danni's place with Allen and Danni slept with Darryl last night!"

I couldn't believe my ears. "You're still married, Cat. That's adultery." Then what she said really sank in. "Danni slept with Darryl? Geez."

"I didn't want to waste time. Strike when the iron is hot is my motto. Plus Danni needed cheering up. She was really down over those incest memories."

"She was depressed and you sent her over to screw your husband! Do you realize how crazy that sounds?"

Cat shrugged. "Danni wants him."

"What does this have to do with the confrontation thing?" I asked, still shocked, but wishing Cat would get to the point.

"Danni's loved that fool a long time. I appreciated how she always kept her distance and respected our friendship. I know that after I kick Darryl's sorry ass to the curb, somebody will snatch him up soon, because the motherfucker is too helpless to wash his own drawers. I figured the woman who should have him should be Danni."

"You make the most insane shit sound almost logical," I said.

"It is logical. Danni wants him to move in with her, and I'm dying to have my apartment to myself, but we couldn't figure out how to do it without, you know, Darryl getting a clue. He'll freak if he knows we set all this up together and may even dump Danni out of some wounded male pride bullshit, so we decided that I'd discover them both in bed and throw a fit. Then I can throw him out, and he'll move in with Danni. Sweet, huh?"

I stared at Cat and rubbed my temples, a headache starting to form behind them again. "What makes you think I want to involve myself in this adulterous freaky mess?" I asked.

"Because you're our best friend," she said, looking angelically innocent.

I snorted.

"I can't wait to get back into the single life. Winston and I are going partying to celebrate afterward."

"With Winston all you're going to see is the gayer side of KC," I said.

"Yeah, but it's a start."

She got up and headed to the door. "Be at my place at eleven A.M. sharp. I'm counting on you. We don't have long because Mrs. Thompson can only babysit a few hours longer, and I want to get at least most of his crap out of my place before I hit the streets tonight."

She was out the door before I could say a word in protest.

I looked at my watch and frowned. Cat wasn't giving me much time to deal with the notion of the confrontation thing either. I'd bet money she did that on purpose.

I stood outside Cat's apartment door at eleven. I saw her coming down the hall with a shopping bag in her hand.

"Come in when you hear the screaming," she whispered, and

let herself quietly in. I rolled my eyes and followed her into her apartment, because I couldn't resist wanting to see all of the spectacle to come.

Danni and Darryl were lying in the marital bed in a postcoital state.

Danni stared at the clock next to the bed, obviously waiting.

Then simultaneously, Danni shrieked and Cat yelled, "You sorry motherfucker!" at the top of her voice.

I swear that Darryl jumped three feet in the air. Hmmmm, I thought Darryl would be better endowed. He was aw'raht, but nothing to write home about.

"How could you?" Cat said, her face wracked in anguish as she approached the bed. She was a damn good actress. Danni, however, wasn't. She looked as if she wanted to giggle.

"I gave you six years of my life!" Cat howled.

The look on Darryl's face. Oh, Lawd. I have never seen a man look so terrified. He was a fireman for chrissakes and Cat was barely five-foot-two. He looked as if he were facing a firing squad of Marines.

"Please, honey. Cat, calm down," he said, his voice wavering and cracking as if he'd entered puberty last week.

"Don't tell me to calm down when you're fucking my best friend!" Then she turned on Danni. "What do you have to say for yourself, you treacherous white bitch!"

Danni lost it and started cracking up laughing, but buried her face in a pillow to make it look like she was crying.

Cat dropped her shopping bag, and pulled out an automatic weapon which looked like an Uzi or something. Had Cat lost her mind?

Then I relaxed because I could see from across the room that the thing was plastic. But Darryl looked like he was going to puke.

112

Cat was being plain evil. One thing about that girl, she didn't just get mad, she got even.

"You are going to pay for every second I wasted with your sorry hind-end," she hollered, accompanied by the classic neck swivel.

Cat raised the gun and squinted at Darryl. "Get on your knees, motherfucker, and prepare to face your maker."

"Noooo, no, no, no," Darryl started blubbering and bawling. Then he actually pissed himself.

"What the fuck?" Danni yelled, as she leapt out of the bed to avoid being splashed with pee.

But Cat didn't relent. Girlfriend had some serious anger pent up.

"On your fucking knees or I'm going to blow your head off," she screamed at Darryl again.

"Cat? Don't—" Danni started to say.

"Shut up, white girl," Cat thundered. Danni shut up.

"Now, say you're sorry," she said to Darryl.

"I didn't intend to sleep with her," he said, tears running down his cheeks.

"Didn't intend to sleep with me?" Danni said, frowning and tightening the blanket around her.

Cat eased up 'cause I could tell she didn't want Darryl's big mouth to screw up her arrangements.

"I don't give a damn who you screw, motherfucker. Start apologizing for all the shit you put me through for the past six years. Start with how you made me feel like shit, asshole! Then follow up with every time you disrespected me, you punk bitch. And you can finish with every goddamn time you sat on your ass and expected me to clean up for you, motherfucker." She opened fire at his face, shaking with fury.

Darryl screamed like a little girl before he realized that a stream of water was hitting his face.

"And I put ice in it, you no-good fucking dog!" She directed the spray toward his genitals, but I doubt it was possible to shrivel them more.

"Get your clothes on and get out of here so I can get the hell on. Get out of here and don't come back or I'll swear I'll shoot you for real."

She turned the water pistol on Danni. "You too, white girl. Get out and take your piece of shit with you!"

Danni was practically already dressed and Darryl scrambled. "Wipe yourself off first, fool," Cat yelled at him. He grabbed the sheet with shaking hands and wiped himself off. He dressed with shaking hands, and Danni hurried him out the door. She looked back at me over her shoulder and gave me thumbs up. I'd never see a woman look so pleased.

After the door shut behind them, Cat started giggling.

I shook my head. Danni and Cat were some mean bitches.

But it was some funny shit, I had to admit.

CHAPTER 12

Return, return, O Shu'-lam-ite; return, return . . .
—Song of Songs, 6:13

I'm a colossal jerk. I didn't control myself from tasting her. I said the V-word, vampire. I scared Luby away.

Stupid, stupid. I didn't think I'd come to this backwater town and find the woman that I had to have—and keep. When I saw her in the elevator that day, the most beautiful woman I'd ever seen in my life, exotic, feminine and glowing violet, scarlet and golden, blazing with power. I couldn't believe it.

With my luck, it figured that she didn't have a clue about what I was and who she was. There was no way I could resist drawing Luby in and making love to her and then finally, making her mine despite the distraction of Alyssa's constant onslaughts.

I was still tangled in one relationship and did the equivalent of marrying another woman without her consent on extremely short acquaintance. I must be mad.

I even suspected Luby of tricking me, of being fully aware of her power and casting an obsession spell that I couldn't detect. I'd drawn a seer's mirror and seen that there were no such influences over me. Luby's spell was of the natural sort, embedded in her sexy body, beautiful face, appealing quick-witted personality, and loving heart. She'd caught me on her line and drawn me in to the point where I was flipping and gasping for air.

Women loved me so readily, I thought my own heart was immune. I knew that down deep I was glad that I was as capable as the next guy of wanting a woman for my own.

But now I had to wait. I needed to be patient until she came to me out of love and not fear. There was no way that I was going to let her go, but to force her with fear could destroy the hope I had of her truly loving me.

Not only lusting for my body, but loving the soul of me too. I wondered if I'd ever experienced that from any woman outside of my family. I doubted it.

The waiting was necessary, but too painful.

I reached out with my mouse and checked my e-mail to distract myself. Five e-mails from Alyssa. I deleted them all without reading them.

The last three years have been hell. The novelty of irresistibly attracting women wears off soon, let me tell you. I couldn't work out in the world as I used to anymore, traveling to ranches within a fairly large territory, looking after the animals. Women sniffed me out like mosquitoes sensing blood. I had to move back in with my family and become a virtual recluse. I'd actually looked forward to marriage, thinking it would relieve my loneliness.

I promised to mate with Alyssa, a pledge bond between her family and my family. When she came to the ranch to meet me, she fell for me in the shallow way women often do.

When she begged me for sex, I obliged, hoping to rid her of the unseemly habit of staring at me, following me around, and

116

hanging on to my every word like she was a dog and I was eating steak.

My decision to appease her was a terrible mistake, because it turned her superficial crush into an obsession. Most men may think that having a wife who thinks they are God's gift wasn't a bad thing, and at first, I also supposed it could be worse.

It did get worse, far worse. *Love me, love me* was her incessant cry, not having the sense to know the heart can't be ordered into compliance. I know that I treated her with respect and tried to be friendly, but gods, I couldn't take a breath without her tearfully accusing me of not loving her. What was I to do? Lie? I wonder if that would have satisfied her and shut her up. I doubt it.

Eventually, she allowed herself to be deceived by the demons and became their tool in a misguided attempt to force me to love her by magical means.

She wouldn't return to her home, but stayed in our family home moping and having tantrums. At the end, I told her it was over and left my home, heading for the airport and buying a ticket for the first city I got a flight to.

My sister, Elaine, gave me books on magical arts to figure out and repel the spells and demonic attacks that she thought Alyssa would pursue me with. I disregarded her concern and figured that with my absence, Alyssa would get over me and move on.

I was wrong. Elaine's books were worth their weight in gold. My ex-fiancée completely lost her mind. I tried to reason with her, tell her that my attraction is an effect of magical phero-mones that I have no control over.

I tried to explain to her that without the glamour, I'd be an ordinary man, no better than any other.

She wouldn't believe me. She thought if she could force me to love her, she'd be happy. When I told her if she isn't happy within herself, my love wouldn't matter in the least, she looked at me as if I was insane and burst into tears. She swore an oath that she'd get me to love her.

Did I mention that she was out of her mind? I'm sure I did. Gods, I wish that woman would get a life.

In the midst of this mess, I saw Luby and lost my heart for the first time in my thirty years.

The wards I'd set for protection against magical intrusions shrieked. Alyssa sent another demon.

"You busy?" the demon asked, putting down a cigar. It was the lizard-looking demon Alyssa usually sent. The demons and I were becoming too well acquainted.

"Sort of," I said uncomfortably. "I was getting ready to do some writing." You can understand why I dislike pissing demons off, but it was getting more and more unavoidable.

"This won't take long," he said. He unrolled a scroll that trailed the floor. "She wants me to read this poem she wrote." He looked pained. "I'm sorry man, but she won't unbind me until I do it."

"It's that bad, huh?" I said.

"Excruciating." He cleared his throat. "How do I love thee? One. You are a rain-washed flower bloom in May. Two. You are a fragrant and soft green meadow of hay. Three. You are the sunshine that lights up my every day. Fo—"

"How many are there of these?"

"Almost a hundred," he said apologetically.

I swore and headed for the bathroom. I decided I needed a shower.

The demon stood outside the door and droned away. I didn't turn off the water until after his voice ceased and I was sure he'd faded away. The woman must be resorting to torture.

I craved the heat so I turned down the AC and put on soft silk pajama bottoms and left my shirt off.

I settled back down at the computer and clicked over to my favorite gaming site with the idea of killing a couple of hours in mind.

There was a light tap at the door and I knew instantly that it had to be her. My mouth dried. How could one small woman make me so nervous? I hurried to the door.

She stood on the threshold, looking anxious, harried and utterly desirable, I had to stifle my urge to gather her small body into my arms.

I stood aside and motioned that she enter. "I wondered if you had any leftovers?" she asked.

"No, but I can whip up a sandwich," I said.

"That would be delightful."

She followed me to the kitchen and sat at the breakfast bar, perched on one of the stools I'd recently purchased. "Want a beer?" I asked, trying to take my cue from her and keep it light and casual.

"Thanks."

She raised the beer to her lips and I opened the refrigerator, determined to make her the best sandwich known to man. "Do you like mushrooms?" I asked.

"I love them."

"How does Portobello mushrooms, rare roast beef, and Swiss on sourdough sound?"

She giggled, her pearly teeth flashing white. "It sounds like food fit for angels right now." She relaxed. "I spent all afternoon and evening helping Cat move Darryl's stuff out of their apartment."

"They're separating?" I asked, pouring olive oil in the pan to sauté the large mushroom cap. Luby and I had a lot to address, but I liked to indulge in small talk in the intimacy of my kitchen. I appreciated how Luby instinctively realized that we needed a space to reconnect before we tackled the issues ahead. Alyssa was certainly not capable of such subtlety.

"Yes. And you won't believe what happened. Cat decided she wanted to give Darryl to Danni and she set it up to catch them in bed and threw him out."

I raised an eyebrow. The activities of mundane humans seemed to be as dangerous and bizarre as any magicks. But I decided not to question her on the matter further because I was far more interested in her activities than those of her friends.

She cleared her throat as I was cutting a Bermuda onion into the thinnest possible slices.

"Can I ask a favor of you, Jake?"

"Anything."

"Do you mind putting on a shirt? You're somewhat distracting."

I quelled a grin. I didn't relish turning on random women anymore, but I loved turning her on. I set the knife aside and washed my hands. "I'll be right back," I said.

I debated changing my bottoms because I wasn't wearing briefs and was aware that the outline of my manhood was clear in addition to the slightest sign of my arousal being extremely evident. I decided against it. With Luby, I needed all the help I could get.

She'd gotten a second beer out of the refrigerator when I returned and was looking tense again. I quickly finished putting her sandwich together and presented it to her.

She bit into it and appeared to melt. "Mmmmm, this is so good."

Gods, she turned me on. I couldn't take my eyes from her mouth. She ate like she made love, with free enjoyment and gusto. She demolished the sandwich in a few minutes.

"Yummy," she said, and I had to hold my hands behind me to keep from grabbing and kissing her.

She took the plate to the sink and rinsed it.

"You want to listen to some music or watch television?" I asked. I didn't care what we did, as long as she didn't leave.

She wiped her hands with a paper towel. "I'd like to talk, actually."

I nodded and let her lead the way to the living room couch.

"Grandma talked to me yesterday. What she had to say was more than unsettling."

I waited, suspecting the revelation she'd been given.

"She talked about faith, about magic, a little about my father and about you, Jake."

I raised an eyebrow.

"She . . . she said there is no such thing as vampires."

"I agree," I said.

"But you said you were a vampire. And you bit my neck!"

I felt bad about that. There was really no excuse. "I said I was like a vampire. I—my family, we have an affinity toward the blood of certain people."

"Your family drinks people's blood?" She sounded a little alarmed, but not as alarmed as I would have in her situation.

"No. There's an affinity for the blood of people we love. It's not that we drink it. You could say we're drawn to taste it."

She looked like I'd hit her in the stomach. I hurried to explain further. "When your blood is hot and rushing under me in the midst of our lovemaking, you smell like the sweetest floral nectar possible. It's like a drug, the way you feel and taste, and I lost control." I studied my bare feet, not knowing what else to say. "I'm sorry," I added.

"You said you . . . " she said, so softly I could barely hear her, still looking stricken.

121

"Excuse me?"

"You said you loved me."

I looked away from her questioning eyes. I wanted this revelation to happen at a different moment, one with roses and music and romance, not the present uncertain moment of our relationship. But it happened now and I couldn't take the words back. "I do," I said.

Her lip trembled. "You love me?" she whispered again with something like wonder in her voice.

"Always." And I threw caution to the wind and stilled her lips under mine. She wound her fingers through my hair, while I kissed the tracks of tears running down her cheeks. I picked her up and carried her to my bed, because anything else had ceased to matter.

CHAPTER 13

Thou hast ravished my heart . . .
—Song of Songs, 4:9

I lay Luby gently on my bed and unbuttoned her blouse and let it fall open, tracing circles over her hot, fragrant skin with my tongue.

She shivered. "Jake, yes."

I stilled her lips with my own, reveling in the sensation of her petal-soft lips. I tasted longing, need, and a touch of fear. Did she fear love? Herself? She mustn't fear me, not ever.

"You must know how beautiful I think you are," I whispered in her ear. My breathing was ragged, uneven. I brought myself under control. I wanted to worship the temple of her body, her precious gift to me.

I twisted my fingers through her cloud soft hair. We whispered nonsensical love words to each other, promising eternity.

I made love to her mouth, feeling her tongue sensuously moving against mine. She moved against me restlessly, seeking, wanting . . . rubbing her softness against my hard straining cock that wanted nothing more than for me to pull her bit of panty aside and sink into her to the hilt. My desire ached to break free and flood her.

Her hands traced the length of my cock through my pants and I gritted my teeth to maintain control.

"I want your dick inside me," she said, her voice husky with sex.

I drew in a quick breath. "Baby, we've only begun."

I trailed kisses down her neck as I unhooked her bra and slid her blouse off her shoulders.

Her nipples rubbed against the soft material of my T-shirt and she tugged at it, craving skin against skin as much as I did.

I pulled the shirt over my chest and groaned as she rubbed her hard nipples against mine.

Her breasts were beyond perfect, full, high and tender, the nipples budlike and sweet. I bent to suckle them, eager to feel their softness against my tongue. I teased them into hard brown peaks with my lips, flicking her sensitive nipples with my tongue until she moaned and moved under me.

"Ohhhhh, that feels so good," she whispered.

I eased her denim skirt and panties over her hips and she reached under the waistband of my pants and grasped my aching rod. Her small hand could barely reach around it and my body stiffened as she circled her thumb over the moistness seeping from my opening.

"You set me on fire, woman," I said, tossing her shirt and panties over the side of the bed. I ran my fingers through her soft cottony curls, claiming her secret places for my own. I couldn't wait to feel her sweetness quake and convulse under my mouth.

I kissed the swell of her soft belly and entwined my fingers further in her trimmed triangle of curls, my mouth and lips working lower as I held her straining knees open.

"I need to taste you." I dipped my tongue into her moist slit. Tremors of pleasure shook her body as I fastened my mouth on her tiny bead of pleasure and sucked gently, rhythmically.

She writhed and bucked, her hands grasping my hair. "Yes, yes, yes," she moaned. She went wild against my mouth, her hips riding the wave. Her sighs and moans intensified to sharp gasps, and I felt the waves of pleasure convulse her body. I moved up and watched her face, beyond beautiful in ecstasy.

I could wait no longer. I rolled off the bed and dropped my pants to the floor. I hefted myself in my hand offering it to her. Her eyes devoured me. With a quick movement, she took me into her mouth, her tongue rotating around the head of my cock. I'd soon explode if I didn't get inside her.

I eased out of her mouth, every nerve ending on my cock screaming in protest, covered it with a condom, and gently moved between her legs, my cock rubbing against her wet folds.

"Please," she whispered. "I want you inside me now." She reached for me. I pinned her arms over her head.

She laughed and wriggled under me until the tip of my dick grazed the opening of her damp pussy. I kissed her hard, my tongue thrusting rhythmically into her mouth. She bucked against me harder, the walls of pussy pulling me in.

It felt so good, every muscle in my body tensed. "Please," she begged again.

I slipped it into her hot wetness a fraction of an inch, holding back with every fiber of my being from burying my cock into her tight walls to the hilt.

She tossed her head back and forth frantically against the sheets. "Fuck me, fuck me, do it, dig that big fucking dick into my pussy," she gasped, thrusting her hips while she ground against my meat, her muscles working to suck me in.

Goddamn. A man could take only so much.

125

I surged forward, filling her tight pussy so I gasped and she screamed. I lost control, thrusting my cock in deep and fast in and out her slick walls. Her pussy tugged and massaged every inch of my cock, while I gasped against her mouth.

She met my passion with her own, our bodies colliding again and again while I pumped her hard and hot, a freight train running wild. Her pussy clutched and gulped my straining cock until there was nothing but the red of my frenzied passion as I beat my cock into her body, climbing, climbing, climbing, the pinnacle so close, I could feel it.

Then she stiffened, and her pussy snapped against my cock as she called my name. I cried out in response, my seed exploding from my body. I pumped into her wildly, the spasms taking me harder than they ever had before.

Her fingers clutched my shoulders when I finally sank into her, completed, and knowing more than ever, I wasn't going to let her go.

Both of our skins were sweat-slicked. I raised my hand and the overhead fan came on. The breeze wafted across our bodies. "It's not too cold for you, is it?" I asked Luby.

"No, it feels good." She kissed the side of my neck, and snuggled up next to me with a happy sigh.

I hated the thought that we'd ever have to leave this bed.

"You didn't bite my neck?" she asked, touching it.

"No, I didn't. The way it was between us was so strong right at the first, that I barely knew what I was doing at the time. But now I'm aware . . . It won't happen again."

"I'd probably let you if you wanted to, anyway," she said. "I never felt you do it anyway."

"No. It's not right. We should share blood in a mutual, controlled way."

She sighed. "Everything is bizarre. My grandmother told me that my father was a Santería priest from New Orleans. She also told me that my mother killed him."

I blinked. That was a heavy revelation to lay in there among many. "Why?"

"That I don't know." I felt her almost imperceptible withdrawal and wasn't surprised when she changed the subject. "Tell me about your family."

"It's big. I have one other brother and three sisters. I'm the oldest. There are tons of aunts, uncles, and cousins there too. My grandparents live at the ranch big house, which serves something like a family headquarters. There are other houses scattered around it, including my parents'. It feels something like a village or a tribe much of the time."

"I can't imagine," she said. "I'm an only child. My grandmother raised me."

"Your mother was imprisoned?" I asked, since she said her mother had killed her father.

"No. She stays in a home for the mentally ill."

Her mother was severely mentally ill. That explained why Luby was reluctant to deal with the unseen world. She must fear what happened to her mother would happen to her.

The wards screamed again and I almost audibly groaned. The timing couldn't be worse for the demon to appear. I wasn't worried that Luby would perceive it—demons were careful not to be perceived by the mundane, so it wouldn't expect me to respond in her presence. But the damn things always hang around forever if they think there would be an opportunity to see some sex. They were as a rule, terrible voyeurs.

"She wants to know what you thought about her poem," the demon said. "I was kind and said I had no idea." The demon licked his lips with a forked reptilian tongue as his eyes raked over Luby's body. "Nice. Can I touch?" He reached out a scaly hand toward Luby's breast.

"No!" I said.

"What?" Luby said. "What do you mean, no?" She lifted herself up on her elbow and looked around.

Her eyes widened and she let out a shriek that pained my eardrums. She scrambled over me out the opposite of the bed from the demon, grasping a sheet to her naked body.

"I do believe the witch sees me," the demon said, pleased.

CHAPTER 14

. . . the little foxes that spoil the vines
—Song of Songs, 2:15

"Oh, God. Christ in heaven save me! What is it saying!"
She turned to flee and I caught her and held her.

"Do you see the demon?" I asked, trying to be calm.

She looked at me as if I'd lost my mind. Then looked over at the demon who puffed on a cigar and seemed as if he was enjoying the spectacle immensely.

She opened her mouth but nothing came out. Now the demon was pantomiming that she drop the sheet. Asshole.

"It won't hurt you," I told her.

"But it's a demon!" she shrieked. "Lemme go."

For a small woman she was very strong. "I thought the poem sucked," I growled to the demon. "Begone!"

It grinned and vanished.

Luby's knees buckled and I picked her up and put her back on the bed. She immediately tried to run from the room again. I pinned her to the bed with my body. "Will you calm down, woman? It's gone."

"But it's a demon! A demon! Let me up, dammit! I'm out of here. I'm not fooling with any fucking demons!"

So feisty. Gods, she was hot.

"Demons generally can't hurt you without the direct aid of other humans—or be seen, because they're unable to affect matter on this plane. Usually only highly trained mundanes and magical humans can see them." The fact that she saw demons both excited me and made me fear for her. I didn't think she was ready to take on the reality of the unseen world. The demon referred to her as witch, the catchall term for a person with a genetic magical strain.

"Luby, listen to me. Your grandmother told you about the special abilities that some people have and that they're genetic, right?"

She nodded.

"I know she told you that you're one of those special people. You have to calm down and open your mind because once your abilities mature, you'll see all sorts of things you don't readily understand."

Her lip trembled, but I could tell she was pulling herself together.

"Tell me about . . . demons," she asked, "Why was that thing here? And why was it smoking a cigar?"

"They have bad habits too. I have been meaning to tell you something anyway."

"You're a Satanist right? You call up demons and worship them?" Her face twisted in disgust.

"No, never. What I've wanted to talk to you about is my ex-fiancée, Alyssa. She's the one who keeps sending this demon to me."

"You were engaged?" The news seemed to make her almost as unhappy as the notion of demons.

"It was an arranged marriage, mainly a joining of families. She'd moved to my family home, but we had yet to set the date for the bonding ceremony. She fell in love with me, but the feeling was never mutual. I broke off the engagement right before I left Montana. She refused to accept it and leave my home, so I left."

"That's why you came to Kansas City? To get away from some woman?" Luby asked.

I nodded with a grimace. It sounded cowardly when somebody else said it.

"She sends demons to you for what?" Luby asked.

"To relay messages or to execute spells. I've been able to block both demonic and long-distance spell casting, but I can't stop the messages—or the messengers. I know there are ways to secure your dwelling against demons, but I don't yet have the knowledge or skills to do so."

Luby looked as if she wanted to throw up again. "What sort of messages?"

"Um, pleading for me to come back to her, general vituperation and reviling, love poetry, stuff like that."

"She has demons read love poetry to you?"

"Yeah, he hates it. She's a terrible poet."

Luby was silent.

"Are you okay?" I asked.

"I guess so. I'm still trying to wrap my mind around a cigar-smoking demon reading you love poetry from your lovesick ex-fiancée."

"It's bizarre, all right. I've been hesitant to confront her, because first, I think that would make it worse, and second, I think that's exactly what she wants."

"Can—can demons come into my home?" Luby asked.

"I suppose they can, but why would they want to? Like I said, they can't affect you directly. They can only work through other humans, and it's very important to them that their existence not be known to mundanes."

131

"Why do you keep calling us mundanes? It sounds like something out of a Harry Potter novel."

"Those were Muggles."

"Oh. Why don't demons want their existence known? Because it would scare us?"

"They like to scare you. No, it's because if most humans believe in them, then they'd believe in the unseen world. They'd believe in the Most High and the magic of the universe and humans would try to wield it in great numbers."

"That's not a good thing?"

"Not to demons. They're the enemy of humankind. It would mean outright war, a war that they might not win. They prefer working behind the scenes, using subtle influence to destroy humanity."

She chewed her fingernails, something I'd never seen her do before and she still looked shell-shocked.

She got out of bed. "Will you come with me? I want to take a shower. I don't want to be alone in this apartment anymore. Actually, I don't want to be alone anywhere anymore."

She was subdued and showered quickly. I could tell she didn't want me to join her, so I spent the time shaving. I showered afterwards while she stood in front of her bathroom mirror and tried to run a brush through her luxuriant tight curls.

Afterwards, we sat on the couch, the noise of the television filling the background.

"Why did I see the demon now, when I never saw any before?" she asked.

That was a good question, one that I'd been pondering. "You have ingrained natural magic. Our people can innately perceive the hidden world, and if they can't in their youth, they generally do when they come into maturity at age twenty-seven."

"That must be what Grandma meant when she said that when I turned twenty-seven, things would change."

"Probably. Whatever our innate ability, it usually becomes manifest around that time."

"I'm not going to be twenty-seven for two months," she said.

"Still, it's around the time."

She was fidgeting, clearly anxious. "What sort of natural abilities do you get? What will I be able to do?" She gave a weak smile. "Manufacturing money out of thin air would be a good one."

Poor baby. Here she was trying to joke and she was obviously terrified. I gave in to impulse and pulled her to me. "I don't know what you'll be able to do, but if it's anything like you, it'll be wonderful."

"What happened to you when you became of age?"

It was my turn to feel anxious. My gift wasn't wonderful at all. "I attracted people sexually."

"This is a new thing for you since age twenty-seven?"

I nodded, embarrassed.

"No wonder you're so weird about it."

"I'm not weird about it."

"Yeah, you are. You're self-conscious about the hotties who want to launch themselves at your bod, tear your clothes off, and have their way with you. Man, if you were a woman, you could work that gift to the nth degree. I wonder if I'll get something similar"

"You won't." My voice was too sharp, but the thought of every man out there vying for her considerable charms teed me off.

She laughed and stretched in my arms. "When I'm with you, I can deal with all this crazy crap, although the idea of demons does freak me out. It feels as if you've lifted a huge weight off me."

She looked at her watch and picked up my remote. "Uh-oh, I'm missing my favorite show, *Hot Suburban Mamas.*"

She leaned into me, her gaze fixed on the television.

For her, I'd even sit through an episode of *Hot Suburban Mamas*.

I got up while Luby was still sleeping beside me to cook breakfast. It was good to cook for someone so appreciative of my culinary skills.

I overdid it. I made strawberry blintzes oozing with cream cheese, sausage, ham, fresh fruit salad, and strawberry muffins.

Luby emerged following her nose. Her huge grin when she saw the spread made it worthwhile.

"Are you working on getting me fat as a pig?"

"Nope, but you would be as cute chubby. Sit, I'll serve."

She dug into breakfast with open pleasure. "You know what I always have for breakfast? Coffee and toast or coffee and cornflakes and milk. This is restaurant caliber eating." She cleaned the last bite off her plate and patted her stomach.

"I'm late for work," she said, looking at her watch. "I have a meeting this morning."

She stood and dropped a light kiss on my forehead. "I have to run."

My mouth full of blintz, I nodded and said, "See you tonight."

I heard her open the front door. She gave a blood-curdling scream. I knocked over the chair in my haste to get to her, the food I'd just eaten sour in my mouth.

She was doubled in pain just outside my door, vomiting up her breakfast. The demon stood beside her, a broken bottle of some potion at her feet.

Alyssa had attacked the woman I loved, using the demon as the means to deliver her evil potion.

CHAPTER 15

It was but a little that I passed from them . . .
—Song of Songs, 3:4

"I'm sorry, man," the demon said. " I had to tell the other witch about your new squeeze and now she wants her dead." He shook his head. "You should have said you liked the poem."

I snarled and hauled Luby over the threshold, slamming the door in the demon's face. Luby was gray and moaned in agony, clutching her stomach. "It burns," she said, gasping. "It burns bad."

Fury and fear shook me and I picked up the phone and called home. I had to have help. I closed my eyes and prayed my mother or father would answer. My prayers were answered.

"Hello," my mother said.

"This is Jake. Listen, because I have no time."

I heard Mother draw in a breath. "Okay, Jake," she said.

"Alyssa magically attacked a young woman I've been seeing. She sent a demon with a potion. The woman is in severe pain. Please, help me, Mom," I said, aware of the naked pleading in my voice.

"I was afraid something like this would happen," Mom said. "Bring her here as quickly as you can. Her life depends on it."

"What if she dies?" I had to force the unbearable words through my teeth.

"Induce a trance in her that will slow down her bodily functions and your father and I will work protection in transit to stabilize her. Tie a violet ribbon around both of your right wrists."

Thanking the gods that Luby was light, I grabbed my wallet and her purse, stuck my feet into a pair of sandals and carried her at a dead run down the stairs, channeling the power and mumbling an incantation that would still and slow her body.

I burned rubber to Kansas City International Airport, swerving into a Walgreens on the way to buy purple ribbons as instructed. If anybody could save Luby, my mother could. Her magical knowledge was at a sorceress's level.

My cell phone mike was stuck in my ear and my credit card on the dash as I raced down the highway, begging the travel agent for the next available flight in the shortest time possible to Butte, Montana. By the time I pulled in front of the terminal, our tickets were waiting. We'd have to make a connection, but the flight was the one that would get Luby help quick.

I underestimated the difficulty of airline travel while carrying an unconscious woman. I requested a wheelchair from the skycap and gave him another $100 to park my car. I carried her from the car and placed her in the wheelchair, but she kept falling over.

"Your lady friend looks a little worse for wear," the skycap said with raised brows.

"She's fine. She suffers from . . . narcolepsy." I rushed her through the terminal doors, trying to hold her upright with my one hand.

The lady at the ticket counter kept looking from me to Luby nervously. She took forever to get our tickets and the plane was boarding in a few minutes.

Luby nearly slid out of the wheelchair when we finally got the tickets and I started to rush to the gate. I was pulling her up and trying to arrange her arms when two uniformed airport security guards approached. "Can we have a word with you, Mister?" one asked.

"I'm afraid not. We might miss our flight."

Then I noticed that they both stared at Luby oddly. "She has narcolepsy," I explained.

One of them put his hand on Luby's neck. He soon snatched his hand away as if he'd been burned. "She's dead!"

"Of course she's not dead," I snapped. "She's disabled. Check her pulse again."

The other man had already lifted his walkie-talkie, presumably to call the authorities. "Try it again, Ted," he ordered.

The security guard made a face and touched her neck again.

"She has a strong, regular pulse," I said, putting all the power of suggestion I had into it.

"She does have a pulse, Oscar," he said. I exhaled in relief as I saw Oscar lower his walkie-talkie.

"Are you gentlemen going to make us miss our plane because of your discrimination against my disabled girlfriend? I'm going to report this to the Narcoleptic Society of America!" I said, making sure my tone was appropriately loud and dripping outrage.

They blanched. "No problem," said Oscar with the walkie-talkie. "Hurry on to your flight and take care of her."

I hurried off to the gate with what I hoped was the proper indignation.

I'd bought first class tickets. The flight had almost completely boarded. The flight attendant checking our boarding passes looked at Luby in consternation. Her head had completely lolled back in her chair. I pushed her head upright. "She's a disabled narcoleptic," I said, and went past her up the ramp. "I'll leave the wheelchair right outside the plane," I called behind me.

Outside the airplane entrance, I picked her up and carried her to our seats. As I labored to strap her she did look dead. My fellow first class passengers gaped at us.

I finally settled down beside Luby and took her hand in mine, trying to think about how I was going to manage to change planes in Denver rather than the awful possibility I could lose her.

Four hours later, I bundled her into a rental car to drive to the ranch, three hours away. I prayed to every god I'd ever heard of that I wasn't too late. If something happened to her, it would be my fault. I'd rather die myself.

It was dark when we arrived at the ranch, but my heart lightened to see our houses, their windows glowing yellow. My mother had instructed me to go straight to the big house. They'd had to enlist the assistance of my grandparents and other family members to perform the magic needed to shield us from further attack and Luby from deteriorating on my rush here.

I ran to the door with Luby in my arms. My mother pulled it open before I could knock. My brother was behind her and he took Luby from me. "Follow us," she said to me as he strode with Luby quickly toward the room of rites.

A table covered with dark blue velvet cloth stood in the middle of the room.

My brother carefully laid Luby on the table, then looked at me. "Good to see you back home, bro."

My mother embraced me briefly and then motioned to my aunts and sisters starting to fill the room. "We need to start. There isn't a moment to waste." She turned to me. "We're going to have to ask all the men to leave the room. This is a woman's spell of love and revenge and woman's rites are needed to break it."

"Mom, please save her." I was terrified of what could happen—and of what I would do to Alyssa if it did.

She patted me on the cheek and moved to the table to where my grandmother, aunts, and sisters surrounded Luby with linked hands.

My grandfather clapped a hand around my shoulder and led me from the room.

Sara, the housekeeper, brought us her homemade ale in the great room. I stared into the roaring fire that had been spelled to cast off no heat into the warm summer night trying not to think and trying harder not to feel.

"How long will it take?" I asked.

"As long as it takes," my father said.

"So who is this woman?" my cousin, Lim, asked.

"Her name is Luby. I met her shortly after I arrived in Kansas City." I took a deep breath and decided now was as good a time as later to tell them. "I've taken her as my bond-mate."

There were quick indrawn breaths, along with frank gasps.

"Let me get this straight," my father said. "Alyssa, your legally betrothed, was here driving us crazy for over a year and you did not choose to bond with her in all that time. We understood."

He glared at me. "You went to Kansas City and meet some woman to whom you pledge a lifelong troth after a few days' acquaintance. Are you mad?"

I picked up my ale and took a swallow while I nodded. "Mad crazy about her," I said.

"Mundane, I suppose," my grandfather said wearily, his voice heavy with disappointment. A mundane woman would dilute the bloodlines we tried hard to maintain.

"No. She's one of us, but has little family and isn't yet aware of all it means."

"If she were mundane, she'd be dead by now," my brother added.

"She saw the demon that attacked her, but I don't believe she can hear them, at least not yet. She's only now maturing into her abilities."

"Many times those not raised in one of the families end up mentally unstable," my grandfather said. It was not a kind statement, because several of my uncles and cousins had been brought into our family from a solitary existence.

I didn't want to think about Luby's mother.

"She has a family now. Us," I said flatly.

"I disapprove of you taking a woman before you finished with Alyssa," my grandfather said.

"I tried. She wouldn't listen to reason. She won't quit pursuing me. Now she's attacking the ones I love."

"Were you cowardly? Did you make the break clean, and tell the woman you didn't love her and that you'd never bond with her?"

My eyes narrowed. If any of my cousins, my brother, or possibly my father asked such things at this time, I would have lashed out at them. But respect for my grandfather, the patriarch of the family, ran deep. "I did. She didn't believe me. She thinks she can force my hand and my heart."

Grandfather gave a sharp nod. "I observed the woman's self-absorption while she was here. I wanted you to assure me that you had conducted yourself in a worthy way. You and this other woman have my blessing."

He stood to leave, tall and straight, belying his many years. "As soon as the woman has recovered, you will leave her here so we can protect her while you finish your business with Alyssa."

"I doubt if she'll stay. Her life is in Kansas City," I said to grandfather's retreating back.

"If she wants to have a life left to live at all, she'll accept our protection," my father said.

CHAPTER 16

Whither is thy beloved gone
—Song of Songs, 6:1

"What the fuck?" I was flat on my back on a hard table shadowed by a passel of white and Asian women hovering over me holding hands.

"Jake said your name was Luby," said a handsome woman who seemed to be in her forties. The only reason I didn't catapult off the table and head for the door was because her eyes were exactly the same green as Jake's. She had to be a relative.

She extended her hand, "My name is Beth. I'm Jake's mother. She indicated a woman who looked to be in her mid- to late fifties. "This is Jake's grandmother, Helene Kosevo."

Then she went around the circle introducing each woman in turn, Jake's aunts, Jake's cousins, Jake's sisters. There was no way I'd ever keep their names straight.

It was a testimony to how freaked out I was and how polite I was trying to be that I didn't immediately demand to know why they were standing around my black ass on a table in a strange room.

"You have been very ill," Beth said after she'd finished her exhaustive introductions. "What do you remember last?"

I mentally floundered. Then I remembered the white-hot pain in my stomach. It had felt as if the acid juices had seeped out and burned me from the inside out. Then I remembered that awful scaly demon thing leering at me and throwing a black liquid at my stomach from a bottle that he then broke at my feet as his fanged mouth silently laughed and laughed.

I started to cry, because if this is what being crazy was like, it sucked balls worse than I thought.

Helene handed me a handkerchief. "You're safe now, child," she said. The other women started to leave the room.

"How long have I been here?"

"About forty-five minutes. You were under the spell of a powerful potion. It took all of us this long to break it," she said

"Um, how long have I been unconscious?" I looked around wildly. "Where am I?"

It's almost nine P.M, Monday evening. You're in the Kosevo family home in Rosebud County, Montana," Beth said.

"Montana, how did I get to Montana?"

"By plane. Jake brought you to us to save your life."

I knew I could barely cope with the implications of what was happening, so I chose to focus on the small things I could manage. "Is there a phone I can use?"

"You may use our phone to call wherever you like. I'm going to show you to your room and there's an extension there."

Jake burst through the door, looking tired, scared, happy, and gorgeous. "Thank the gods, you're all right." He reached out and pulled me to him.

"Thank you," I said, brushing my lips on his jawline. "I gather that if you hadn't somehow got me here, I'd be history."

I looked at Beth. "And thank you and the others who saved my life." The memory of the fiery pain and how everything went dark and constricted afterwards shook me. I'd known that I was dying.

I drew my head back and gazed at Jake. "You said the demon couldn't hurt me."

"I said it couldn't harm you directly. Alyssa used it to deliver a potion and curse."

"Your ex-girlfriend tried to kill me? Damn. With a demon and a potion? She doesn't know me from Adam." If I saw that crazy bitch, I'd kick her ass back to hell where she belonged.

"She is obsessed with my son," Beth said. "That's why you need to stay here with us until Jake deals with the threat."

"I appreciate your hospitality, ma'am, but I can't do that. I have a job, bills to pay, things like that."

"You don't need to worry about such things," Jake said. "Your body has been through a lot. You need to take some time to heal anyway."

"I can heal just fine at home."

"If you go back, Alyssa will likely attack again. And the second time you may not be so lucky," Beth said in a quiet voice.

When put like that, Jake's mother had a point. "When do you plan to go and set that woman straight?" I asked.

"Tomorrow."

I nodded. I hated that he was leaving, but it's better to take care of the crazy bitch now than later.

He helped me off the table and my knees almost gave way. I could not believe how sore and weak I was. It felt as if I'd been pounded with a hamburger mallet.

"I'll show you to your room," Beth said, holding out her hand. I took her arm and was glad for it. She gave Jake a sharp glance. "You let her sleep tonight. She's been through a lot."

"I'll see you tomorrow before I leave," he said, giving me a chaste kiss on the lips. I smiled at him and followed his mother as she led me out the door.

I took in Jake's "family home." It seemed to be what I'd imagine a European castle to look like from the inside. There was no Western ranch motif whatsoever. Great exposed dark wooden beams ran across impossibly high ceilings, the floors were smooth white marble with black veins and were spread with rich Oriental carpets.

The walls were covered with oil paintings, some seeming quite old, and with finely woven tapestries. The rooms I glanced in as we passed them were filled with heavy, dark, antique-appearing furniture. Jake said his family was well-off, but that was an understatement. "Your home is lovely," I murmured to Beth.

"My husband and I live close by, in a separate house. Many of these furnishings were shipped from Europe when Jake's great grandparents had this built."

"Fascinating. Where were they from?"

"Croatia. They tired of the big house several years ago and left it to Jake's grandfather. They now have a condo in Florida they love."

My eyebrows shot up. Jake's great grandparents were still alive and in Florida?

Beth led me into a pleasant room, decorated in tones of cheery yellow with a single four-poster canopy bed. It looked like a teenager's room, but very warm and welcoming.

"Sara has put fresh towels and linens and a nightgown out along with a pitcher of ice water. It would be best for you not to eat tonight and have only very light meals tomorrow. I chose this room because it has a private bath next to it, and I felt you'd enjoy that. As I said earlier, feel free to use the phone." A quick smile flitted across her face. "Welcome, and I mean that. You seem to make my son very happy."

I decided that I liked her. I tend to know immediately if I'm going to mesh with another person and Jake's mother and I were going to be cool.

I slipped into the nightgown and took two of the extra strength Tylenol they'd set on my bedside table, and crawled under the covers. The nagging worry whether I would be able to handle demons and other assorted weird shit dissipated for the first time in over twenty-four hours.

I felt Jake's soft touch and smiled at the dream. "Baby, wake up," he said. I opened my eyes and looked into his green ones. "I hate to wake you, but I had to tell you goodbye. I won't make my plane unless I leave now."

I reached out and touched his cheek. "Be careful. Do you know what you're going to say to her?"

A muscle throbbed in his jaw. "I plan to think about it on the plane. My mother told me that if we had to, we'd bind Alyssa's power if needed."

"You can do that? Will it be dangerous for you?"

"I can't, but my mother and family can. I don't think Alyssa would hurt me. But I don't want to strip her powers. I feel guilty enough, you know? The woman is obsessed and miserable. I want to get her to move on with her life."

That he didn't want to hurt that silly woman made him dearer to me. I reached for him and we melded in a tender kiss.

"Take care, I whispered. Jake nodded and was gone.

PART THREE

Things change.
—Alyssa, Luby

CHAPTER 17

I held him and would not let him go
—Song of Songs, 3:4

When Jacob called me in Los Angeles and said he needed to talk to me, it was difficult not to let triumph bubble through my voice.

He'd finally seen reason. All the times I'd been loving and giving, exposing the shreds of my heart in the hope that he'd give me another chance and return to his senses—none of that worked. Destroying that little black slut he whored with brought him to his senses.

I'm sure he realized that I'd done him a favor. The woman was beneath him, a mundane. He couldn't possibly love her. She was only his sex toy and would be quickly forgotten. I know a man has needs. Jacob spent the previous year being tantalized and aroused by my slim body. He was too much of a gentleman to ravish me as often as I'd begged him to. He'd only made love to me once and then put me on a pedestal. He knew I was a good woman, a nice girl.

As soon as he got around some loose woman he didn't value, he probably couldn't wait to—.

I couldn't stop the sobs moving up from my heaving lungs to tear at my throat. Why was I trying to kid myself? I'm a stupid, ignorant, ugly, deformed woman. Who am I to think that the most perfect man in the world could care about me?

But I had him once. The tears came faster. He'd been my betrothed, my greatest and only love. The night he'd made love to me was etched in my mind, the happiest moment in my life. I played it over and over again.

Jacob was always so kind, so unfailingly polite. Until the day he told me that he wasn't going to bond with me, that he wished me to leave.

He was unmoved when I pleaded that he realize that he was having difficulty adjusting to the idea of having a loving life mate, of regular marital sex. He really loved me, he had to. Otherwise I couldn't love him so much, and otherwise how could he have been so nice to me? Why did he put me on such a high pedestal, treating me like a chaste, fragile flower?

My tears dried as rage flew through me. It was entirely his fault I was mixed up with these demons that taunted and made fun of me. It was his fault that I was sleeping with other men in a vain search for something to soothe the pain he caused me.

It was his fault that I was lonely.

After we got back together, he'd have to pay for the suffering he caused me. I might withhold sex every once in a while, make him beg for it. I'd flash my alabaster breasts and he'd go crazy and then I'd tell him I didn't feel like it. My hand crept between my legs as I imagined the hot scenario.

I showed up at the bar early and nursed a drink as I waited for Jacob. He was right on time, and so handsome I could hardly bear it. All the women turned their heads to look at him as he passed. He's mine! I wanted to scream at them.

I slid off the stool to make my entrance. He stood up until I was seated at the intimate table in the corner of the bar. That's a gentleman for you. Every woman there envied me.

"Alyssa," he said.

"It's good to see you. It's been too long." I wanted our time together to be pleasant. There was no reason why we couldn't enjoy ourselves together. I'd begged him to meet me at my place. I could bespell him and bind him to me forever if I could get him on my own threshold, but he'd refused.

"You know why I'm here."

"To rekindle old flames?"

Jacob looked as if he smelled something bad. "No, I'm here because you almost killed an innocent young woman outside my apartment yesterday."

I figured that it would be undignified to deny it. There were traces of me all over that potion.

"She's not dead?" I was disappointed. It had taken a huge effort to mix and spell the potion properly. "I haven't had time to send my demon to check."

Suddenly there was so much fury in Jacob's face that I drew away from him. He looked as if he wanted to murder me.

He leaned forward, his eyes glittering with rage. "What do I have to say to get through to your small and insane mind? Listen carefully to the little words I'm going to use."

"Jake—" I started to protest.

"Shut up. If you do anything, and I mean anything, to harm that woman again, your powers will be bound and you'll become no different than a mundane. If you don't get out of my life and stay out, your powers will be stripped and bound. That includes demons, magic or anything else your tiny mind can dream up. Do you understand?"

I couldn't believe it. Bind my powers? "You don't have the ability," I said.

"My family does and you know it."

"But—but I love you, Jacob!"

"Here is another thing I want you to understand so well that you can repeat it back to me: I don't love you, I never did love you and I never will love you. Never. No matter what you or anyone else does, even the gods themselves. Now, in light of your history of poor comprehension, repeat back to me what I just said."

It wasn't Jacob. It was a simulacrum. Its eyes were hard, its jaw angry, and its mouth disgusted. "You are not my Jacob. I know you're not my kind, perfect Jacob."

"My family won't have to get involved, it seems," he said, his voice hard. He leaned forward and said, "Do you know what the council does to insane sorceresses? My next stop will be to report you to the Families Council if you don't repeat what I told you."

I felt the blood drain from my face. The council would turn me into a mundane. I'd rather be dead. "You said you don't love me and you never will," I said.

"Say, 'And that I've never loved you.'"

"You loved me once, you did!" He was trying to hurt me that's all. He was angry.

"'And that I never have loved you.' Say it!" His voice was harsh and demanding.

"You never have loved me," I said. But I would never believe it.

"Do you understand what will happen to you if you ever seek to harm those I love again? If we ever see or hear from you again?"

"But she was only your prostitute. It didn't count."

He swore savagely. "She's my bond-mate," he said. My mouth dried.

"You lie!"

"No. Don't you see her mark on me?"

I narrowed my eyes and opened my perception. There was a shimmer of new pink in the colors shifting around him.

"And my mark is on her. I'm sorry about your disappointment and pain, Alyssa, I truly am. But you have to move on with your life. Find a man who can love you."

I couldn't respond. I was an empty shell, hopeless and worthless. "You have more than amply informed me that I'm not worth loving."

I got up, hurting so much, I could barely stand straight.

Even then he had no mercy. "Remember what I said, Alyssa. I mean it."

I almost ran out of the bar.

CHAPTER 18

By night on my bed I sought him whom my soul loveth.
—Song of Songs, 3:1

As soon as Jake left the ranch to comfort his murderous ex-fiancée, I picked up the phone to call my office. My boss seemed only slightly worried about me not showing up to work for two days. I simply told him I had an emergency and I'd be taking my sick days.

Danni was almost impossible to reach by phone at work, so I rang Cat at her office.

"Where were you yesterday?" she asked. "Danni and I were almost ready to call the police."

"You're not going to believe this, but I'm in Montana with Jake's family."

"What! You just upped and went to Montana with him, like that? What about your job?"

"I'm taking some vacation. Hey, will you and Danni water my plants while I'm gone?"

"Sure, but how long are you going to be away? This isn't like you at all. Are you sure you're all right?"

"Better than I've ever been. Hold down the fort for me and

give Danni my love." I gave her the number where I can be reached. My cell phone service didn't reach out here to wherever I was in Montana.

I'd saved the hardest for last. I picked up the phone to call Grandma. I didn't worry about whether she'd be home because I knew her routine so well. If it wasn't too hot outside, she'd be in the flower garden, her cordless phone within reach.

She picked up on the first ring. "Hello, baby. How are you doing today?"

"I'm doing fine. Grandma, I have news."

"Oh?"

"I'm in Montana with Jake's family."

"That's good, child. You stay with your young man and his family as long as you need. I'll be fine."

It was beyond weird that Grandma didn't question me. Normally, she'd be upset if I did something as uncharacteristic as up and leave the state with no notice or preparation.

"I did tell you I was in Montana, didn't I?"

"Yes, you did. I've never been there but I hear it's beautiful country."

"Grandma! Aren't you concerned about me?"

"Of course I'm concerned about you, but you just told me you were fine, didn't you?"

Humph. "Yeah, I am."

"I was hoping you'd call me. You know I love you very much, baby, don't you? More than anything in the world. You've been a blessing, such a source of happiness for me."

"I love you too, Grandma. You know that. And I know that you love me."

She sighed. "Sometimes the telling doesn't hurt. Just always do your best and always try to do the right thing and you'll be fine—even in Montana. I'm sorry you never brought your young man around to meet me."

"I'll bring him when we get back. I think it's serious, Grandma. I think he's the one."

"That's wonderful. If your love is pure and clear, it can't go wrong."

Grandma seemed to be in a pensive, melancholy mood today. I wondered if her arthritis bothered her.

"I'm hoping I'll be home by the weekend, but if I'm not, Bea will take you around?"

"She will. Don't worry about me. Take care of yourself, rest up, and mend."

We talked for a few more minutes, but after I hung up, I wondered how she knew that I need to rest and mend? I hadn't told her that I'd been injured.

I took a long shower and put on the robe that was hanging on the back of the door. I couldn't bear to put on the clothes I took off yesterday; they reminded me of the wrenching pain and the sour odor of vomit.

I heard a tap on the door and tightened the robe belt around my waist. A young woman came in the door, her green eyes the same color as Jake's. It was uncanny that so many people in Jake's family had eyes that were so green.

"My name is Antonia," she said. "Everybody calls me Toni and I'm Jake's sister. I think these will fit you." She handed me a pair of overalls, a T-shirt, an unopened package of Hanes panties, and a pair of socks.

"They are perfect. Thank you."

She sat in a chair near the door. "I'll wait until you're dressed and show you the kitchen."

I obediently gathered up the clothes and headed for the bathroom.

I followed her to the kitchen, padding on sock feet. I still didn't feel all-the-way-normal, and I was starving.

"We've all eaten already, but I'm happy to cook you something."

"Some cold cereal with milk would be fine, if you have it."

She smiled at me. Toni looked very young, still in her teens. She pulled a step stool up to the polished dark wooden cabinets that extended all the way up to the impossibly high ceiling, rummaged around a little and pulled out a box of sugar frosted cornflakes.

I ooohed in pleasure. I was starving and I love some sugar frosted cornflakes. I settled at the table with the box and the whole gallon of milk in front of me and dug in. Toni sat across from me.

"We're mostly self-sufficient out here," Toni said.

"What do you mean by that?"

"We have solar and wind power and we heat using primarily wood stoves. We grow a lot of our own food. That milk comes from our cows. If civilization decided to collapse we'd be self-sustaining."

I nodded politely, but sincerely hoped that the collapse of civilization was too far away for Jake's family to earn any props for making it through.

"How long have you known my brother?"

"We live in the same apartment building in Kansas City." I refilled my bowl with cornflakes.

"You seem a lot nicer than Alyssa. It was terrible what she did to you."

I had to agree with that. "Thanks. What is she like?"

"She's pretty. But she's one of those types who act stuck on themselves and snotty, but their real problem seems to be they don't like themselves enough. Do you know what I mean?"

I nodded. Toni talked fast in the excited way teenagers often did.

"I moved to my grandparents' house recently," she continued. "I want to learn to live more on my own. I'm going off to college next year and I to get used to being away from home."

Moving to your grandparents' house within eyeshot of your parents' home didn't seem like much of a move to me. But living in such an environment, surrounded by a loving family your entire life, could make moving to college very scary. "I think you're going to love it," I said.

"You do?"

"Yes. Everybody is in the same boat. I was terrified when I moved from my grandma's house to college. I felt really out of place too."

"Where did you go to college?"

I hesitated. I usually stayed far away from the topic of my education. "I went to Vassar. But my point is that I realized that the other students weren't that different from me under the skin. There were some I couldn't relate to and some who couldn't relate to me, but there were also some who I felt at home with when I was with them and they felt the same way toward me. If a black woman from Kansas City can have a great time at Vassar, I'm sure you will find a lot to enjoy at college too."

I poured another bowl of cereal. The box was getting light, so I peered inside.

"We have more cereal," Toni said.

"I feel like a bottomless pit after almost twenty-four hours without food."

"Jake told Mom that you were a lawyer. Where did you go to law school?"

"I went to Stanford. I wanted to check out the West Coast. I had a good time, when I wasn't studying—but after I graduated, I wasn't interested in any of the prestigious firms. All I wanted was to go back home to Kansas City."

"I think I'll be that way too and want to come back home, no matter how much fun I have at college. I bet you have a great job though."

"No, I just have a job." My superiors at the law firm discounted my education. I heard one partner say I was a living example of affirmative action. I let it go because I wanted to keep my job and be at least somewhat comfortable there. Anyway, I knew I'd worked as hard for my A's as any white person in my class, so fuck him.

The cereal and milk churned in my stomach and sourness bubbled up in my throat as I scrambled to the trash can, barely reaching it in time before all the food I'd ingested heaved up and out of my mouth. Ugh.

It took a while until my stomach stopped doing cartwheels. My head was hung into that trash can so deep, I felt I knew the damn thing intimately.

Toni handed me a cool, damp cloth and a glass of ice water, which I promptly gargled and deposited in the trash can.

"Let me get this mess out of your kitchen," I said, embarrassed.

Toni hesitated. "I'll take care of it," she said. "It's my fault. I should have remembered how sick you'd been yesterday."

"It's definitely not your fault. You didn't shove multiple bowls of cereal down my throat and swallow it. My own greedy self did that. I need another trash bag first so I can double bag this mess, and then point me in the direction of your outside trash can."

"We don't have an outside trash can."

I was at a loss. "Um, where should I put the trash then?"

"We separate it—that's the recyclable plastic bin—and then we either burn it, bury it, use it for compost or recycle it."

"Um, I'm sorry. I think I messed up your recycling plans." I couldn't face washing the vomit off all the stuff.

"We'll bury it. Don't worry about it."

"No, I'll bury it," I said firmly.

"You're sick. You need to go back to bed. You look like somebody wrung you out like a dishrag."

I deflated. I did feel like crap and not up to arguing about doing something I didn't want to do anyway. I insisted in double bagging the mess and setting it by the back door, and then meekly followed Toni back to my bedroom.

I opened my eyes and looked at the clock—it was five o'clock! I'd slept the day away after vomiting in the kitchen this morning. I felt better, as if the long sleep had recharged my inner batteries.

I rolled over, picked up the phone and tried to call Grandma. No answer.

I phoned Cat. "Whazzup, girl?" I asked.

"I miss you," Cat said. "I hate to whine, but when are you going to be home?"

I thought about Jake's crazy ex-fiancée. "I'm not sure."

"That luscious man spoiling you?"

I wanted to tell her everything that had happened and that Jake was gone . . . to set the heifer straight on who sent a demon to throw a potion at me that almost killed me? Naah. "Yes, he's spoiling me," I said. "How are Danni and Darryl doing?"

"Peachy. I'm going to Vegas and get a quicky divorce. Danni is sure he'll marry her afterwards."

"Is Allen adjusting?"

"Shoot, yes. I should have done this earlier. He's blossoming with a real man around the house. Follows Darryl around like a puppy dog. But I have news to tell you!"

The caller ID clicked. I let it go, feeling guilty because this wasn't my phone. I'd have to get Cat off the line.

"I decided to go back to school," she said.

"Wow, Cat. All these changes at once. Are you sure it's wise?"

"I was admitted before. I was going to major in social work."

Social work? That didn't sound like Cat.

"But I chose to marry Darryl after graduation instead." She sighed. "So this is more like getting a portion of my life back, you know? I'll be moving to St. Louis and staying with my sister there. I'm planning to start in January."

"So soon, Cat?"

"I'm ready to make a change."

"It seems as if we're all making changes," I said. We were moving apart, going our separate ways so fast it seemed as if we were ricocheting off our own desires, speeding away from each other.

"Change happens," Cat said.

I cleared my throat. "I can't tie up this line long."

"I understand. I can't get over you letting that man drag you away like that. I think I like him."

"Yeah, me too," I said.

Cat chuckled. "You've changed a lot more than we have," she said.

If she only knew.

I'd just put the phone in its cradle when I heard a light tap on the door. "Luby?" Beth called.

I rolled out of bed and grabbed my robe, feeling guilty that I wasn't up and dressed. "Come in."

Beth entered and handed me a piece of paper. "There was a

164

message on our voice mail for you to call that number immediately, that it's urgent."

I thanked her and frowned at the number. I didn't recognize the number or the name, Gabriel Zita. The only people who knew I was in Montana were my grandmother, Cat, and Danni. Any of them would have called me before passing the phone number on. Still frowning, I picked up the phone.

Chapter 19

The phone rang once, twice. "Kansas City Police Department," a receptionist's crisp voice said.

I could feel the pulse in my temple. "May I speak with Gabriel Zita?"

"One moment, please."

A long moment passed, then another. "Gabe Zita here."

"This is Luby Jones. I'm returning your call."

"Thank you, Ms. Jones. To confirm your identity, could you give me your date of birth, address, and home phone?"

I reeled off the numbers staccato.

"Thank you for your patience. I hope you understand we needed to verify your identity as the granddaughter of Mrs. Lucinda Jones." He paused. "I regret to inform you—"

"No." I hung up, and curled up on the bed, wrapping my arms around the pillow, big gulping sobs starting to work their way up from my gut.

The phone rang again.

And again.

I wailed into the pillow, it pressed hard to my face and curled in the smallest ball possible, but I still didn't think I could bear the pain.

Grandma dead? And without me by her side? No, no.

I don't know how much time passed until someone pulled the pillow away from my face and eased me into a sitting position, holding a cool glass to my lips.

"Here's some water," Beth said.

I obediently drank. I felt numb, as if I'd died inside too.

"The policeman told us about your grandmother. He said you hung up on him."

I nodded. I had to see Grandma to know it was true.

"I have to leave now," I told Beth.

"I know. We've reserved a flight for you already. Jake's brother will drive you to the airport in an hour."

I didn't have any luggage, nothing but my purse and the skirt, blouse, and sandals Jake's family had kindly given me for the trip. I managed to call Cat and Danni and they both said they would meet me at the airport. My body went through the motions that would get me back home because I couldn't believe that Grandma was gone until I saw it for myself. I drew in a quick breath on a sob and blew my nose. Tears leaked from my eyes unexpectedly all the way back home.

When I landed at Kansas City International Airport, as soon as I walked through the gate, my friends rushed up and embraced me murmuring condolences.

"Is Jake coming?" Cat asked.

I nodded. He'd told me that he was changing flights to Kansas City. "He'll be here in a couple of hours. I've got to see Grandma. Please take me to her."

Danni nodded. "The police want us to take you to the morgue to identify her body and sign the autopsy releases."

"Why does she need an autopsy? She was an old woman."

Cat and Danni looked at each other uncomfortably. The pause grew too long. "She was murdered," Danni said.

I pressed my fist to my mouth to keep from crying out and nobody said anything else as we made our way to the car. I was almost blind from the tears streaming from my eyes. I couldn't take this, I couldn't. It hurt too much.

They wanted me to view my grandmother through windows or with cameras, but I insisted on seeing her.

They made us wait in a little white room with cinderblock walls and cheap linoleum. I stared at the clock. It was almost three A.M., a surreal hour when all but the most staunch partyers and nightshift workers slept. I shivered, although I knew the room was close and hot.

"Ms. Jones," a man said. We all started to follow him, and he raised his hand. "They need to wait here for you," he said. I followed him to a cool place where the foul odors were covered with harsh disinfectant.

He moved to a black shape on the table and started to unzip it. It only hit me then that this was Grandma, in a black plastic bag in a cold, ugly room. I shook harder, feeling the vibration through my entire body. He exposed Grandma's face, her dear face. I touched her cheek one last time and gave a cry at the cool, alien texture. This wasn't Grandma. A disembodied voice said, "Who do you identify this person as?"

I stared at her one more time, a lump filling my throat to bursting. "Lucinda Jean Jones," I said. "My grandmother, Lucinda Jean Jones."

There were two people, one on either side of me as they escorted me out of the room. They needn't have bothered because Grandma taught me well how to carry myself under

169

strain. *You're a lady, Luby. Remember that and it'll get you through all sorts of mess.*

They took me to a man who helped me into a chair beside his desk. "Do you have any other relatives?" he asked.

"My mother is mentally ill. How—how did she die?"

"She was stabbed twenty-seven times," the man said. I heard nothing else after that.

Danni and Cat got me home and let me into my darkened apartment. Danni checked my messages and Cat undressed me as if I were a child and put me to bed. Then Jake was there, gathering me in his arms, rocking and rocking me while I sobbed against his throat.

I woke up in my own bed, tangled in Jake's arms. Warm happiness thrummed through me until I remembered. Grandma was dead, gone forever. Icy grief worked its way up to my throat and a sob escaped.

He caught my mouth in a perfect kiss, tender and full of shared sorrow.

"Make love to me," I whispered. "I need to feel alive."

"Nobody ever dies, love. We only change," he said.

His hands started to play me as if I were an instrument, his lips moving over my skin. I licked his neck, tasting honey and smoke, the fragrant deliciousness that was Jake. His fingers moved into my cream-filled cleft, scissoring my clit. I spread my legs and moaned as hot, wet pleasure welled through me. For these moments I could forget. I needed him inside me. I needed to feel the life of him.

I moved over him and reached for his hard penis and covered it with my own juices, rotating my pussy lips over its plumlike head. I felt him tremble.

I impaled myself on his blood-filled shaft, shuddering with the pleasure.

I moved in rhythm with the beat of my heart, frantic and fast, his thick dick stroking the slick walls of my pussy like a piston. I leaned down over him and kissed his lips, not slowing the pumping of my hips. His fragrance filled my nostrils, my body was full of him.

He rolled me over in a quick movement, sinking his thick cock deep within me, stilling my hips. "Baby, I was going to spill. Damn, you make it hard to hold back." I wriggled around him, contracting and releasing my pussy on his dick.

He moaned and pulled out almost to the tip.

"Give it, give it to me, give that dick to me."

He obliged, plunging into my pussy hard and deep making me spasm with delight as he pulled out slow again.

My hips bucked to get filled up with that sweet dick again.

His teeth flashed in a wicked grin.

He worked it, moving his rock hard cock in and out with a grind on the downstroke on my clit.

My face was buried in his neck and he pumped hard, the ridges of his big dick head working my walls and beating against my cervix.

I was never more alive, I thought as the convulsions made me scream and jerk as the pleasure took me so hard the edges of my vision went black and pleasure so sharp it was etched in anguish as pussy pulsed and trembled around his dick.

With a roar he plunged in deep and shuddered, I felt his seed within me, full of life, roaring and mixing with every cell of my body.

My eyes closed in the wonder of it. It had been intense before, but this was incredible.

It was only then I realized that my mouth was full of the delicious taste of his blood.

I looked at Jake's neck in horror. Blood trickled down from a sharp cut. I tested my incisors against my lower lip. They didn't feel long or fanged, but they felt razor sharp.

A small smile played over Jake's lips. "You are bound to me forever and you are truly one of us."

"My grandmother was talking about snake people. Can you turn into a snake? Can I?" Talk about truly. I truly couldn't imagine anything more disgusting. Then it hit me what Jake had said. *You are bound to me forever.*

"What do you mean, bound?"

"We can discuss it later," he said, his voice soothing. That meant he didn't think I could take whatever bound meant on top of what happened to my grandmother. It must not be good. What Jake didn't realize was that I could barely take breathing on top of what happened to Grandma. I couldn't be pushed over the edge, because I fell over it right after that cop said those words to me over the phone, *"I regret to inform you . . ."*

"We can discuss it now," I said. "How am I changed?"

"You're twenty-seven. It's your time, a natural thing. The power is maturing, awakening and thrumming within you."

"The blood thing, Jake."

"We like the blood of our mates. It's how we bond. We mingle our life forces, we mingle our blood. Maybe you can consider it another form of sex."

Somehow I felt let down. "Is that all? No weird powers, no nightshift hours, no monotonous liquid diet?"

He grinned at me. "You'll get some sort of power, if you haven't already. I see it in your aura. Even if you didn't, since you're of the blood, you have the ability to learn to see and manipulate magical energies."

"Of the blood?"

"You have the blood of the ancient ones running through your veins, as do I. You are witch-born." My eyes widened. He wasn't telling me anything I didn't know already or suspect, but the words *witch-born* chilled me.

He sighed. "I have something else to tell you. Remember when I asked you to drink my blood in the wine? I shouldn't have done it. I should have discussed it with you first, but it was as if I was driven. I had to take you."

"What are you talking about, Jake? Please, please get to the point."

"You're my bond-mate. It's like a wife. We're bonded forever. Um, that means permanently. Breaking the bond is a bit of an ordeal."

"What do you mean by that?"

"We can't mate with anybody else. The magical bond won't allow it."

My eyebrows shot up. "And how can this magical bond be broken?" I was crazy about the guy, and the idea of a fidelity bond pleased me down deep, but he had the nerve to do something like that without asking me first?

He flushed. I cocked my head. I'd never seen him change color in the face before.

"Generally, uh, normally it can only be broken, uh, if—"

"If what?"

"One of us dies or turns evil."

"Evil?" I asked.

"There's a polarity between good and evil. They repel. Bond-mates must both be relatively good or evil."

"So opposites don't attract in magic land. Who says what's evil and what's good? What would have happened if I was evil and you bonded with me?"

173

"The universe decides. If we weren't both good, the bond wouldn't take."

"Humph. Isn't it customary to ask first? What about the big, giant rock you're supposed to present me? What happened to the over-priced ordeal of a wedding? What about my cake and my fucking wedding presents?"

He winced. "Don't yell. We can do all that."

"I never was in to all that crap anyway; the point is why didn't you ask like a normal person? What's wrong with you?"

He flushed deeper and concentrated on the knuckles in his hands. "I knew I wasn't going to let you go."

I fell back on the pillows. "You're not getting out of giving me a rock," I said.

He whooped and scooped me close to his body. "You said yes!"

"Like you gave me a choice, Negro."

He looked at me, astonished, and then cracked up laughing.

I didn't mean to say Negro. It slipped out. The grin I was holding back broke over my face. Somehow Jake always hit me with what I needed at the right time. A binding promise, security and forever love at the darkest moment in my life.

My scalp prickled and I looked around, seeing nothing. But somewhere, somehow, I knew Grandma was pleased.

CHAPTER 20

. . . jealousy is cruel as the grave
—Song of Songs, 8:6

Jake and I pulled up in front of the mental health facility where Lily stayed. Jake helped me from the car. I didn't spurn his arm because I felt that without his support, I'd fall over.

He'd taken over, meeting with the police, visiting the funeral home, making the funeral arrangements with Grandma's pastor. I never leaned on a man before. It felt strange, but good.

Jake and I were going to the woman who gave birth to me, and I'd tell her about the death of her mother.

Lily lay in bed watching television. I stepped toward her and froze. For the first time in my memory, Lily looked directly at me.

Before I could open my mouth, she said, "She's gone."

I sat in the torn, vinyl chair next to the door. It smelled faintly of urine and I shifted uncomfortably. "Yes, Grandmother passed away. And I need to tell you that she was—" I took a deep breath. "Murdered."

Lily's mouth dropped open. "You killed her instead of me?"

Her fingers twined and intertwined with each other in a complex pattern. "It made sense for you to kill her. She was older, lived her life. They said you'd only kill one of us. I thought it would be me, knew it would be me. You killed her instead." Her lips spread in an awful rictus. "Thank you," she said.

"I didn't kill anybody," I said. "Especially not Grandma." I wished that Lily had died in her stead. If it had been within my power, I would have done it without hesitation.

"But you did. If it weren't for you and your stud here, she'd still be alive. It's almost as if you wielded the knife and slammed it through your precious grandmother's flesh. Twenty-seven times, twenty-seven times."

I stood, sickened. "Let's get out of here, Jake."

He studied my mother intently, his eyes gleaming like shards of green glass.

Her voice lowered, roughened as if there was a snake lodged in her throat. "I escaped him, but I didn't escape his curse. He told me that my child would be the instrument of death, that it be the cause of the matriarch to die in agony and a wash of blood. All these years I thought it would be me." She spread her lips again. "Mama wouldn't let me kill you. Your grandma protected you. I tried plenty of times. Now, I bet Mama wishes she'd let me."

"You sick bitch," I said. I'd always thought people who cursed their parents were lower than low, but that woman on the bed wasn't my mother. I refused to acknowledge the connection.

"You dare!" My mother's pupils constricted, becoming yellow snakelike slits. I scrambled back, almost falling to the floor.

Jake caught me in his arms.

Her impossible snake's eyes glared at me. The hairs rose on my arms.

"Let's go," Jake said quietly. He pulled me from the room. "She has demons."

He rushed me into the clean, sweet air. I didn't want to ever see that woman again. But a sense of duty still stirred within me. She was all the family I had left. "What do you mean, she has demons?" I asked.

"She's possessed."

"Shouldn't we send a priest to do an exorcism or something?"

He gave a tight shake of his head. "For her, it wouldn't help. You see, she wants to be possessed. The demons are her family, her children, and her lovers. She would resist fiercely."

He drove to my grandma's house silently, his jaw tight. I realized that I didn't care about Lily. She'd chosen her demons over me, and that was the way it had been for a long time. Grandma was my real mother, the woman who raised and loved me.

She'd been killed in the alley behind our house, when she took out the trash. I should have been there, I screamed in my head. Twenty-seven times, oh God, twenty-seven times.

The police had no idea who did it, no murder weapon and no motive.

When he pulled up at the house, it looked as if its spirit also fled. I couldn't bear to see it that way. I couldn't bear to go in either. "Let's drive past," I said to Jake.

"Wait in the car. I need to go in." I handed him the keys.

I leaned back on the leather seat. He'd left the car running and the AC on. I locked the doors after he'd left. Twenty-seven times. Grandma, how did you bear the pain?

After a while, Jake came out looking grim. "I think I know who killed your grandmother," he said.

I waited.

"I believe Alyssa did it," he said.

"Why would Alyssa kill my grandma?" I asked, stunned.

"There are psychic traces of her all around. She had to do it herself. A demon couldn't stab a human directly."

177

"One threw that potion readily enough."

"The potion was magic, not entirely of this plane."

Something flared within me, something hot and ugly, something that wanted to kill. "Where is Alyssa?" I asked through stiff lips.

"I'll contact my family as soon as we get home. We'll stop her." He looked at me. "I never believed she could do anything like this. The attack on you was motivated by bitter jealousy, but what she did to an innocent woman for no reason but vengefulness—it was pure evil. If I'd known she was capable of—"

"Don't blame yourself," I said. I meant it. Alyssa killed Grandma all by herself.

Grandma's funeral was overflowing with people. Her church, her book club, her garden club. I never knew Grandma had so many friends. I'd filled the chapel with white lilies, Grandma's favorite flower.

Grandmother's pastor went to pick up Lily and came back crestfallen, saying she refused to come. He had that indignant air of the well-cussed out. Who knows what Lily's demons had done to him?

Grandma had left instructions for her funeral. She'd wanted it simple. She'd even picked out the casket, one of the least expensive models. She wanted me to carry her Bible to the funeral and she wanted to have the first two books of the Song of Solomon read.

"An unusual choice," the pastor had said.

There's nothing sinful, about passion, child. If you find it, consider yourself blessed and keep the flame alive for as long as you can.

"It's *her* choice," I replied. He said nothing else.

She didn't want eulogies or fuss. She wanted prayers, silent ones from the heart. That was all. I did one thing for her that she hadn't asked. She didn't ask for white lilies, her favorite, or any flower, but I was happy I could do this small last thing for her. The lilies' fragrance was sweet and heady.

The casket was closed. I felt no need to have it open for people to gawk at the meaningless flesh that housed Grandma. Her spirit was long gone.

The pastor was reading the beautiful cadence of the Song of Songs. The words flowed over me and I opened Grandma's Bible to follow along. There was a paper tucked in between the pages, parchment thin and filled with Grandma's flowing handwriting.

I smoothed the letter open.

My dearest child,

I wish there was some way to make this easier for you. We are only given an allotted time here on earth, and when that time is up, the saddest thing is leaving the ones we love behind—for a short while.

Your mother is lost and has been for a number of years. I only wish I could have stayed longer to watch over you.

Sometimes we're tested, but the way out always lies down the right road of faith, forgiveness, humility and most of all love.

Trust in the power of love, for it is stronger than death, stronger than anything.

Never forget that, and you'll always be in the light, instead of the darkness, like your poor mother. You have all my love forever.

May the Christ keep and protect you,

Your grandmother,

Lucinda

Tears dripped off my nose and I fumbled in my purse for a tissue. Jake handed me one and I took it gratefully.

Grandma knew she was going to die and accepted it. She told me to forgive, but right now it was beyond me.

The pastor asked for the silent prayer my grandma had requested, and I bowed my head.

The grief didn't break through my skin until they put her into the cold, dark earth. Somehow, Jake sensed me crack and gathered me in his arms to hold me together.

Then I heard a whisper. *"The earth is our cradle baby, nothing to fear. My body returns to earth, but my spirit flies free."*

I trembled so hard I almost fell. "I heard her," I said. "I heard my grandma," I whispered in his ear.

"Maybe that's your gift. Like your mother, you can hear the spirits." He held me tight.

I could hear spirits like my mother? My crazy, possessed mother?

No.

Danni, Cat, and I sat in my living room for the last time. The movers were coming to put everything in storage tomorrow.

We ate Chinese, but our former camaraderie was an absent guest. Our lives no longer touched one another.

"Cat, I've never properly thanked you," Danni said.

"For what?" Cat dug through her carton with chopsticks and proudly hoisted her catch, a shrimp, before she popped it in her mouth.

"For Darryl."

"Honey, you did me a favor. Aren't I doing much better now? I mean, really?" Cat asked.

I smiled at her and Danni nodded.

"Much better," Danni said. "So am I. Darryl is just the man I needed."

"I knew it," Cat said. "Didn't I tell you?" she asked me.

"You told me," I said. "Danni, I have something to ask you."

"Spit it."

"I wonder if you and Darryl would be interested in taking Grandma's house."

"How much are you asking?" Danni didn't look up from her Chinese food.

"Actually, I was going to give it to you if you wanted it. I thought I'd put it in your name alone."

Danni raised her head slowly. "You're kidding me, aren't you? You need to put it on the market. That house is in a nice neighborhood and I bet it'll be snapped up. I know you could use the money, hell, anybody could—"

"Danni, shut up," I said. "I'm giving you the house and I don't need the money. What I'm asking in return is that you discard or give away my grandmother's things. Keep what you like. I—I haven't been able to face doing it."

Danni bounded over and hugged me, her eyes moist. "You two have done so much for me, Cat giving me her husband, you giving me a house. It feels like I don't deserve to have such great friends."

"You deserve anything good that comes your way," I said. "All of us do."

"It isn't like we're giving you anything we actually want," Cat said. "Get a grip."

"Bitch," Danni said, mustering up a smile through her tears. She turned to me. "This means everything to me. Darryl's credit is poor and I don't know when we'd be able to save up for a down payment."

When Danni mentioned Darryl's credit, Cat looked guilty and got mighty interested in her carton of Chinese food. The state of Darryl's credit probably had more than a little to do with her. Cat was terrible with money.

But I said nothing at all, because I realized that I could see

181

Danni's aura, shimmering with earth colors. I looked at Cat and saw hers too, fiery in tones of blue, orange and white.

I ached with all I couldn't share with my friends. The gulf between us was more than distance and new men, it was the entire unseen world.

If I confided in them, the likelihood would be that they would think I'd gone insane, following my mother's footsteps. If they believed, what could knowledge of a world they couldn't perceive do, other than scare the bejesus outta them?

"I know who killed my grandma," I said, and immediately wanted to clap my hand over my mouth.

Both Cat and Danni stared at me. "Have you turned him in?" Danni asked.

"How? Did he threaten you?" Cat asked simultaneously.

"No, to both of you. And it's a she, Jake's ex-fiancée. She tried to kill me too. That's why I took off to Montana with Jake."

Their jaws dropped to the ground. Their faces sagged, speechless.

"Why did she kill your grandmother?" Danni asked.

"Because she wanted to hurt me."

"She must be a stalker," Cat said. "Are you taking precautions? What's to stop her from trying to get you again?"

"You're just telling us this now?" Danni asked, incredulous.

"We just figured it out recently," I said.

"She's on the run? Is it a federal case since it's across state lines? Is the FBI on it?" Cat asked, her questions rapid fire.

I cast about for plausible answers that didn't involve magic, demons or the like. "Yeah, she's on the run."

"Jake's ex-girlfriend tried to kill you, actually killed your grandmother and you're sitting here all nonchalant. What's the matter with you?"

One of the best things about being a woman is that your buddies generally won't give you weird looks when you unleash a storm of emotion.

My tears were angry ones. The futility of my having to sit around and do nothing while rage stormed inside me was killing me. Jake said his family was binding Alyssa's powers, but that wasn't enough. I wanted her blood to run like she made my grandmother's blood spill. I wanted her to scream in agony. The binding seemed to be no punishment for her crime.

I sniffed. It smelled like tobacco smoke. A misty trail of smoke emanated from a dark corner of my living room. The lizard demon that had attacked me, sat in the darkest corner of the living room, propped up by pillows. "No, don't scream. We don't want to scare your friends, would we? They might think you're, you know—" He twirled a finger at his temple. "Crazy."

CHAPTER 21

Let him kiss me with the kisses of his mouth . . .
—Song of Songs, 1:2

I'd never heard the demon speak before. I'd only seen him. His voice was raspy, nonhuman.

"We need to get out of here now," I said, panicked.

"What's wrong?"

"I smell smoke! Get your purses, c'mon." I grabbed their hands and urged them toward the door.

My panic must have been contagious, because I ran down the stairs, two at a time, with Cat and Danni on my heels, feet flying to Jake's apartment.

His door was unlocked, thank God. He was at the computer.

"What's wrong, baby?" he asked.

"The lizard thingie. It was in my apartment."

"The fire department wants to know the location of the fire," Cat said. Damn, she'd already called the fire department?

"What fire?" said Jake, worried.

"What lizard thingie?" Danni asked.

Oh shit. "Cat, tell them there's no fire," I said.

"Then, why did you say that there was a fire?" Cat asked.

"There was a fire-colored lizard thingie and I panicked," I said.

"You had us run like the demons of hell were after us because of a little lizard?" Danni asked. She'd got it exactly right with the demons of hell simile.

"It wasn't little. It was huge," I said. Somehow, confessing to seeing a demon in my living room to my friends was harder than I thought.

Cat was looking at me, eyes narrowed. "You say there was a huge fire-colored lizard in your living room?" She turned to Jake. "What's this about your fiancée killing Luby's grandmother and almost killing her?"

He looked taken aback. "Luby almost died, yes," while casting an incredulous look in my direction. "By the way, Luby, my mother gave me the means to make my home secure against . . . lizards."

"What about when I go outside? What about them?"

"Lizards aren't going to hurt you," Danni told me, looking puzzled.

"Giant lizards, murderous ex-fiancées. You've been under a lot of stress," Cat said.

"You have," Danni said. "You've suffered a tremendous loss. Maybe you should get some rest, and then if you don't feel better, see your doctor. You might need a prescription."

Great, Danni thinks I'm crazy, too.

The gulf between me and my friends inched wider.

"I better get back home and see what Allen is up to with Darryl," Cat said.

"I've got some errands, too." Cat gave me a quick hug and drew back, studying my features. "You take care of her, you hear?" she said to Jake. "She's a special one."

"I know," he said.

After the door closed behind my friends, I leaned into Jake,

186

absorbing his strength. It wasn't his looks that I loved most about him, although even thinking about the way he made love made me crazy-hot. I loved his sweetness and stability. There was a stable core inside of him, solid and strong, that was as real and tangible as his skin.

I've always known I was blessed. I've never felt unloved. My grandmother loved me well. And now Jake did. For a moment I imagined how it would feel to lose his love. I don't know if I could survive it, but I wouldn't run around killing folks, all crazy and jealous.

"Stop thinking," he whispered in my ear. "Your beautiful face is all frowned up. I can almost hear your brain ticking. Everything is going to be all right. I talked to my mother right before you and your friends came over and she said Alyssa's binding is almost done."

He kissed me, savoring me slow and easy. "I want to make love to you." His voice roughened. "I want to fuck you now."

I let my body answer. We hit the floor in a tumble, passion blazing up like a flash fire. He reached into my jeans and ribbed the crack between my legs through my panties. "Your panties are dripping wet."

"You do it to me, baby."

Then he did it to me some more. His fingers delved into me, explored, and probed, his fingers split in a V-shape and rubbing each side of my clit, but not touching it. My hips rotated with his fingers' steady rhythm inside my moist cleft.

I wanted to see him, taste him. I unzipped his pants and pulled his cock out. I wrapped my fingers around his dick and cradled his tight balls with my other hand.

Closing my eyes, I licked my tongue around his tip. Jake moaned and ground his hips forward to push his hard cock in my mouth. I let my tongue swirl around the veins of his dick until I reached the head. I pressed my tongue against the slit, tasting his salty juices.

As I stroked his dick with one hand, and gently held him cupped in my hand with the other, my tongue worked the head of his cock until I felt him trembling.

Unexpectedly, he withdrew and turned me around. He pulled my jeans and panties down in a swift motion, and slid the engorged head of his cock from my dripping clit all the way to my pussy.

He eased inside me, and I shuddered with the goodness of it. My pussy clutched at him and tried to pull him in but he held me still. I was frantic to feel his big dick pounding inside me.

Jake slammed his full length inside of me, and then slid almost all the way out, leaving only the head inside of me. Then he slid his cock deep again. "Ah, shit baby," he said.

He reached around and his fingers played with my clit, while his slick dick pumped in and out, working my pussy. The sweet friction was driving me wild. I contracted around him, milking it, wanting to feel him shoot his life essence into me.

I felt the storm gather and when it hit, I broke apart and shattered. I whimpered as he thrust to his completion.

We subsided, our gasping breaths easing into each other.

"We didn't make it to the bed," Jake said.

We were heaped together, covered with sweat and sticky fluids. "Race you to the shower," I said.

A few minutes later, the steamy water cascaded over us, arousing us again as our skin rubbed soap-slick against each other.

My nipples tingled as he rubbed the bar of soap across them, transforming them into hard pebbles. "I'm never going to get enough of you," he said.

I gasped as he trailed the soap over the hollow of my stomach and then to my pussy.

I braced myself against the tiled walls as his large hands slowly stirred the soapy lather all over my hot and throbbing body.

I reached for him and wrapped my legs around his waist. I wanted him inside me again. My pussy was empty without that big dick thrusting in and out of it.

He grinned and reached for the showerhead.

Ahhh. My back arced over his strong arm as he directed the strong stream of water to my pussy and took me from cruising to shaking orgasm in thirty seconds.

"That was the appetizer, baby," he said, his voice husky and he lifted me against the tiled shower wall and impaled me on his hard dick.

"I'm going to take you there and back again. You like my cock, sweetheart?" he growled against my throat.

I was beyond words, so I let my pussy answer that question.

Jake and I were getting out the ingredients to cook dinner together. He promised that I'd be a gourmet chef when he got through with me. I wondered if he knew that *edible* was generally the pinnacle of my culinary efforts.

There was a knock at the door. "I'll get it," I said. It was probably Cat or Danni, wanting to tell me something.

I opened the door to a tall, very slim blond woman, with enormous breasts that looked like two cantaloupes stuck on her chest. She was dressed as if she was a Stepford wife or a prom queen, with a sleeveless, pink, calf-length cocktail dress covered with fussy tulle.

"Can I help you?" I asked politely.

"I doubt it. I need to speak to Jake. It's urgent." And she swept past me into his apartment.

Jake was out of the kitchen and in front of me before I could open my mouth to reply. I lifted my eyebrows.

Jake moved in front of me. "Alyssa," he said.

"Jake," she said, wringing her hands.

This was the woman who killed my grandmother? My stomach clenched and I edged to the kitchen. I moved toward the knives with deadly intent.

"They've made me a mundane. I might as well be dead!"

Did she expect us to disagree with her? "I'm going to the kitchen to get the butcher knife to put this bitch out of her misery," I said to Jake, wheeling. "Twenty-seven times," I said over my shoulder, starting to burn with rage as I remembered how Grandma died.

Jake put his hand on my arm. "She's been punished. Look at her. She's pathetic."

"How has she been punished? Stripped of magic? I know plenty of people without an iota of magic who're happy as fucking larks. This murderous, psycho bitch needs to be in prison."

"How am I supposed to live like this, Jacob?" Alyssa asked. "I beg of you, please tell your family to have mercy and restore me! Please, I'm begging you."

I got in her face. "Did my grandmother say please when she begged you not to kill her?"

She raised her head and focused on me for the first time. "Oh, I thought it was you, actually. You weren't at your apartment and my demon couldn't find you, so I assumed you'd be there. That old woman's aura almost reflected yours exactly. It was uncanny. Sorry about that. A little mistake."

Sorry about that? A *little* mistake? I heard a growl rise in my throat as I launched myself at her.

Jake plucked me out of mid-air and held me tight as I struggled, cursed, howled and tried to get to that goddamned bitch. I wanted to stick my nails in her eyes, to kick her in the stomach, and to plunge a knife in her scrawny gut twenty-seven times.

"Calm down," Jake was saying. "Please, Luby, calm down."

"Put the nigger out," Alyssa said, her voice all deep and gravelly.

Jake and I froze and stared at each other. "Okay, now can I kill her? Lemme at her," I pleaded.

Then my breath caught as I saw her eyes flash into the snakeeye slits like my mother's eyes had. Alyssa was possessed by demons too.

I reached out and reached into her eyes with some part of me that I wasn't even sure I had, I grabbed the demon.

Alyssa screamed and fell to her knees.

"What's wrong?" Jake asked.

I knew that I could rip the demon out of her with a mere flick of my will.

But why should I? She deserved to suffer, she deserved to die. My enhanced sight saw past the demon to the fire that burned within her. I could rip that out too. So easy, far easier and cleaner than the bloody effort and mess a knife would take.

Jake swung me around. "What are you doing to her? What can you do?"

Alyssa sank to the floor, indulging in a keening whimper. I wanted to give the bitch something to whimper about.

"She has a demon, maybe more than one," I said. "I can pull it out."

His eyebrow arched. "Since you heard no more spirits, I doubted that was your talent. Getting demons out of people seems to be more useful anyway."

"It will be more useful." My eyes narrowed as I stared at the bitch on the floor that killed my grandmother. "Because I can pull her spirit out also, and cast it to the winds."

I reached out and Jake spun me around. "No," he said.

Fury filled me. "Why do you care about this worthless bitch?

She's a murderer! It was only luck that I'm not dead, and she killed my grandmother. The universe handed me a way to get rid of her without consequences and I'm damn sure going to do it."

"You don't understand," Jake said. "When you take a life, any life, there are serious consequences."

"What were her consequences for her killing my grandmother? She's not looking at prison time. She's not paying a damned thing."

"Yes, she is. The karma from her action could span lifetimes," I rolled my eyes. "Please."

"And it would affect you too if you killed." He took my hand looking utterly serious. "It would affect us."

"Kill me," Alyssa said. I stared at the demons roiling within her. There were three.

"Kill me, nigger. Go ahead and kill me. What are you waiting for?"

She clearly wanted to die. Then I looked again. No, the demons wanted her to die.

"I killed your grandmother, remember? Are you a coward?"

Grandma's words came to me, shining in my mind as if they'd been burned. *Sometimes we're tested, but the way out always lies down the right road of faith, forgiveness, humility and most of all love.*

I knew what Grandma would want me to do. I reached out and Jake screamed in protest. Alyssa's mouth widened in a triumphant grin.

I reached out and felt pulsing energies throb through me along with a sense of exhilaration and power, I'd never experienced before. I pulled the demons out, one after another and tossed them to the streaming winds above to wander, hopefully without cease or rest.

Alyssa collapsed on the floor like a rag doll, unmoving.

"You killed her," Jake said, his eyes wet and bright. "That means our bond will break." He shook his head. "I told you she wasn't worth it."

I nudged him toward Alyssa. She raised her head.

His entire face brightened and he pulled me close. "I don't want to go through forever without you."

A sound emerged from Alyssa. Her entire body shook with the force of her sobs. "I'm sorry, I'm so sorry," she said, gasping and hiccupping. "It wasn't me who did those things. It couldn't be me."

"Please leave, Alyssa," Jake said. "We're done here."

She got heavily to her feet and nodded. She collected her purse and went out the door without a word.

CHAPTER 22

. . . the winter is past, the rain is over and done
—Song of Songs, 2:11

I curled up in a corner of the couch and Jake sat down beside me. We were silent for a while. I was processing the events.

"I wanted to kill her, Jake. I really did. And I had the means to do it in a way that nobody could say I laid a hand on her. The most thorough autopsy would conclude she died of natural causes."

"I know you wanted to kill her," Jake said. "I'm happy for our sakes that you didn't."

"Because killing would tip my balance to evil and our bond would be broken," I said.

He took my hand. "I'm very glad you didn't kill her."

"Grandma stopped me."

He cocked his head and gazed at me.

"Not literally, but I remembered the letter I read at her funeral said that I would be tested, but the right way out was always exercising love. I figured the fear and hatred I felt for Alyssa had little to do with love and I realized what Grandma would have wanted me to do."

"You freed her," Jake said.

"She had three demons."

Jake whistled. "I can't say that I'm surprised. A person has to have an affinity for demonic-inspired actions, or demons couldn't invade their personality. Demons must be invited into one's heart."

I shivered. "Invited or not, they have no place in the human heart."

"I agree." He pulled me back against him. "Is it time to get on with the rest of our life—together?"

"It's way past time," I said.

He caught my mouth in a kiss. After we lifted our heads, I said, "I have one more piece of unfinished business before I leave here."

Jake nodded. Without words, he knew what that unfinished business was.

When I walked into Lily's bedroom, it was a sunny, hot day dragging on the tail end of summer. The familiar negative miasma surrounding Lily filled my nostrils, but it didn't drain and depress me. I was no longer afraid.

"What do you want?" she asked.

"Not much," I said. I reached out and plucked demons from her, screaming and writhing and cast them outward on the air. She had legion. I silenced Lily's screams with a pass of my hand and once I was done, I lit a light in her mind and soul that she might not ever notice, but it would keep demons out. She wouldn't be able to open herself to that sort of invasion again.

A look of perplexed horror crossed her face. "What have you done?" She sat up on the side of the bed, holding the sides of her face as if it was going to explode. "I'm alone. Oh no, no, no, no, it can't be. I'm alone!" Her voice rose to a wail, and I turned to leave the room.

I gave her one final glance. She'd never consider what I'd given her as a gift, but humans were never meant to carry psychic parasites.

I walked briskly down the hall, her wails receding in the distance.

My tread was light, because I knew after all these years I'd finally forgiven Lily for hating me. Her hate had destroyed her, rather than me. When I forgave her, my burden lifted and memories and the taint of Lily were released and dissipated on the winds, like her demons.

When I got back, Jake was waiting with a small black velvet box on bended knee. I whooped and jumped on him, wrapping my legs around his waist. Bonding is great and all, but a big rock and lots of wedding bling never hurt any girl.

"What kind of house do you want to have built on the ranch?" he asked.

"Darlin', do you think I care as long as we're both in it?" I answered.

Jake tilted my chin up for a kiss. "Forever," he whispered, sealing his promise.

"Forever," I said. The truth of the word echoed and reverberated in my heart.

MR. RIGHT NOW

MONICA JACKSON

ABOUT THIS GUIDE

The following questions are designed to facilitate discussion in
and among reader groups.

DISCUSSION QUESTIONS

1. How did Jake's "gift" affect his life adversely?

2. Why did Jake initially propose only friendship with Luby, even in light of their chemistry—the incendiary sex?

3. Why did Luby readily agree only to be friends with Jake? Why did Luby sign on with an online dating service while she was sexually involved with Jake?

4. Do you feel Cat's decision about Darryl and Danni reflect any, all, or none of these characteristics: cowardice, practicality, a lack of love and respect, altruism, caring or a lack of moral values?

5. Why is Danni *only* attracted to thuggish black men?

6. Why is Luby hesitant about white men in general? How does Jake persuade her to open her mind?

7. What are the roots of Luby's lack of understanding and acceptance of her own considerable beauty and innate appeal?

8. Was Luby's grandmother correct in keeping revelations about the "unseen" world, her family's paranormal talents and her own psychic abilities from Luby until the last possible moment?

9. Was Luby's grandmother correct in not telling Luby that Lily killed Luby's father long ago?

10. What did Jake mean when he said that he was "like a vampire" but not really?

11. Why didn't Jake discuss "bonding" with Luby before he did it? How does this show his insecurity?

12. How does Luby's reaction to the "unseen world" and paranormal phenomena reflect her character and growth?

13. Do you think Alyssa shouldn't have been held responsible for her actions? Do you think she went unpunished? If not, what were her consequences?

14. How is Luby faced with a spiritual choice at the end, and how does her eventual choice show her character?

15. Was Luby's final act for her mother an act of mercy or vengeance?